"Where No One Has Gone Before"™

Jeff Katz

STAR TREK®

"Where No One Has Gone Before"™

A HISTORY IN PICTURES

Text by

J.M. Dillard

Additional Material by

Susan Sackett

Terry J. Erdmann

Judith and Garfield Reeves-Stevens

John Ordover

Stephen Poe

Photo Consultants

Paula Block

Tyya Turner

POCKET BOOKS

New York   London   Toronto   Sydney   Tokyo   Singapore

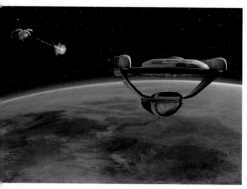

Contents

most beautiful women in Hollywood. This was tough stuff. . . . How about playing a woman in a man's body for a sense-memory exercise?

From these to the jokes we played on one another and the deaths and births that happened as time sped on. It is a fact that I deliberately don't keep photos of events that occur in my life, mostly because, I think, I don't want to see the harsh reality of the passage of time etched in the unforgiving stills.

But here, forced by other hands to see the changes of some thirty years, I peer back into my history with the mixture of a lifetime of feelings. I enjoyed looking at this book for a multitude of reasons. I hope you will find your own reasons to look through this book and enjoy it too.

William Shatner
Valley of Fire, Nevada
June 3, 1994

Tom Zimberoff

For

GENE RODDENBERRY

and all those who, along with him,
have brought the magic of
STAR TREK
to life

Part One

STAR TREK®

THE ORIGINAL SERIES

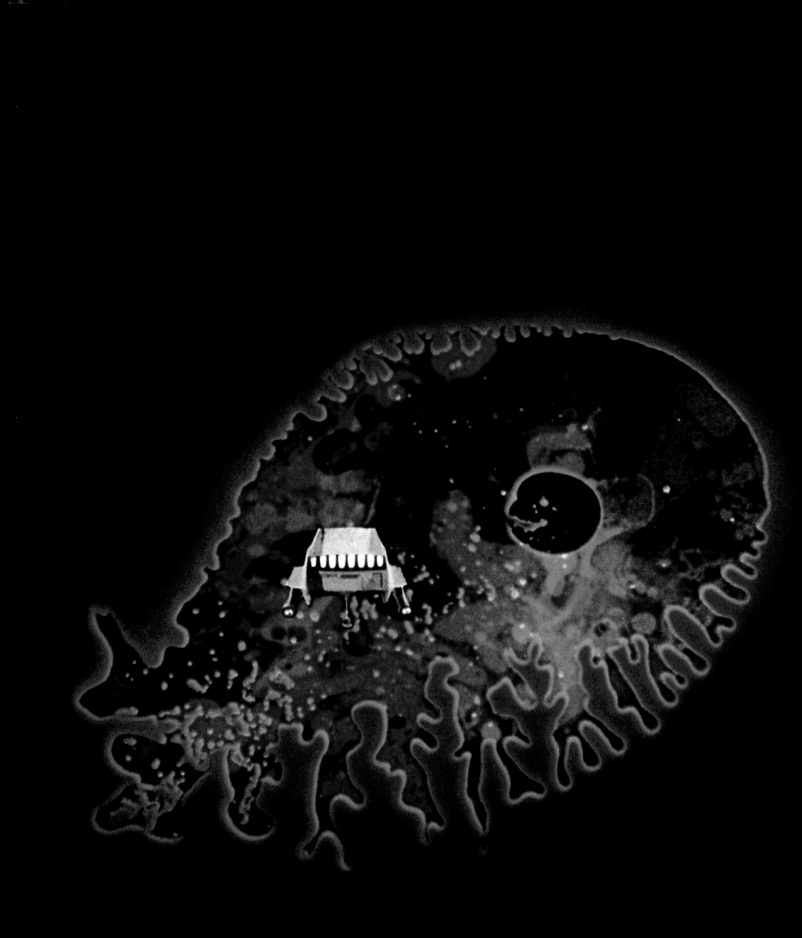

What I principally take credit for is, I surrounded myself with a group of very talented, creative individuals, from the art director, to the costume, wardrobe designer, the actors who took my "skeletons" of Spock and Kirk and really put flesh on the skeleton and made 'em work . . . Television sort of is the exception to the rule that a committee never created anything. The committee in this case does need leadership, but it is a group effort.

—Gene Roddenberry

The story of STAR TREK rightly begins August 19, 1921, in El Paso, Texas, where Eugene Wesley Roddenberry was born. A sickly but imaginative child, Roddenberry read voraciously—Edgar Rice Burroughs's Mars novels, science fiction in *Astounding Stories* magazine. As he grew older, both his health and his imagination continued to improve. Bitten early by the writing bug, he served as a B-17 bomber pilot during World War II, using his off-duty moments to pen aviation magazine articles and poetry, some of which he sold to *The New York Times.*

After the war, Roddenberry became an international airline pilot for Pan American World Airways, but the urge to write never left him. He continued to produce magazine articles and dreamt of going to Hollywood to launch a career as a writer.

In 1949, he gave in to his dream: he quit his pilot's job and moved to Los Angeles, hoping to write for the new medium of television. In the meantime, he paid the rent by joining the Los Angeles Police Department. Even there his talent for stringing words together didn't go unnoticed, and he began writing speeches for then Chief of Police William Parker.

Eventually, Roddenberry procured an agent and began selling scripts to TV series. Soon after, when he realized that he was earning far more as a script writer than as a cop, he turned in his badge and began writing full-time. A number of script sales followed—to "Dragnet," "Playhouse 90," "Naked City," and "Doctor Kildare," among others. In due time, he landed a job as story editor on "Have Gun, Will Travel"; his script for that series' episode "Helen of Abajnian" won him the prestigious Writers' Guild Award.

In 1959, he turned to producing, for as he said, "it became apparent to me that if you want the film to reflect accurately what you felt when you wrote the script, then you have to produce it, too." His first few pilots failed to sell (one of them, "333 Montgomery," starred DeForest Kelley). Finally, he sold the Marine Corps drama "The Lieutenant," which featured Gary Lockwood and Robert Vaughn. (Actors Leonard Nimoy, Nichelle Nichols, Walter Koenig, Grace Lee Whitney, and Majel Barrett all guest-starred on the series.)

"The Lieutenant" only lasted one season, and as it was gearing down, Roddenberry's thoughts turned to his next series—and the future. At that time, he was greatly influenced by a recent nonfiction book, Arthur C. Clarke's *Profiles of the Future*, which discussed "space drive," "warped space," and "instantaneous transportation." Inspired, Roddenberry decided

The man at the helm: Gene Roddenberry on the original *U.S.S. Enterprise* bridge set

Jack Lord

Lloyd Bridges

The Guy Who Got the Job:
William Shatner as the dashing
young captain, James T. Kirk

Casting the Captain

From the beginning, Roddenberry knew exactly what sort of man should captain the *Starship Enterprise*. "Like any writer," he said, "all the characters came out of pieces of me. [The captain] was the sort of eternally cool, resourceful airline pilot I wish I'd been." According to the original STAR TREK bible, Captain Robert M. April, was "about thirty-four, Academy graduate, rank of captain. Clearly the leading man and central character. This role is designated for an actor of top repute and ability. A shorthand sketch of Robert April might be 'a space-age Captain Horatio Hornblower,' lean and capable both mentally and physically. . . .

"A colorfully complex personality, he is capable of action and decision which can verge on the heroic—and at the same time lives a continual battle with self-doubt and the loneliness of command.

"As with similar men in the past (Drake, Cook, Bougainville and Scott), his primary weakness is a predilection to action over administration, a temptation to take the greatest risks onto himself."

Roddenberry clearly knew his character well. But finding the right actor to fill the role—well, that was another matter altogether, particularly since Gene's first choice was unavailable.

"I remember being turned down by Lloyd Bridges of 'Sea Hunt,'" he recalled. "It wasn't a foolish move on his part. I was talking what sounded like a lot of nonsense in those days. He had said, 'I've seen science fiction, Gene, and it doesn't work.' Judging by most of the science fiction around, I had to agree with him.

"We went through a lot of film in casting the part. Jeff Hunter seemed to be about the closest to what I had in mind for a captain."

Best known for his portrayal of Jesus in the film *King of Kings*, Hunter was the last of the principals cast. But when NBC rejected the first pilot, Hunter chose not to return to STAR TREK as Christopher Pike, and Roddenberry was once again looking for a captain. The next person called was Jack Lord, who went on to star in "Hawaii Five-0." But Lord insisted on fifty-percent ownership of the show, and that was unacceptable to both Roddenberry and Desilu Studios. So the search continued and then settled on a young actor named William Shatner.

Shatner was well respected for his work on episodes of "The Twilight Zone" and "The Outer Limits," as well as on an unsold television pilot, "Alexander the Great." When Roddenberry called,

Shatner had just finished a television series, "For the People," and was unemployed. The timing couldn't have been better. Together, Shatner and Roddenberry viewed the first STAR TREK pilot. "I thought it was wonderful," Shatner says. "I saw some of the magic that I thought was a possibility. . . ."

But he also felt that the characters were taking themselves far too seriously. He suggested that it would be better to lighten the captain up. Roddenberry agreed, and so the tormented "self-doubt" mentioned in the original Robert April bio was dispensed with.

Shatner based the character Kirk on Horatio Hornblower, and also on Alexander the Great, the hero from his previous pilot. He says, "Alexander was the epitome of the Greek hero. He was the athlete and the intellectual of his time . . . a great warrior and a great thinker. . . . I saw something of Kirk in Alexander—the heroism . . . [the striking out] into unknown territories."

He also admits that there's more than a little bit of Bill Shatner in James T. Kirk, "if only because in seventy-nine shows, day after day, week after week, year after year, the fatigue factor is such that you can only try to be as honest about yourself as possible. Fatigue wipes away any subterfuge that you might be able to use as an actor in character roles, or trying to delineate something that might not be entirely you. By the second week you're so tired that it can only be you, so I think that in Kirk there's a great deal of me."

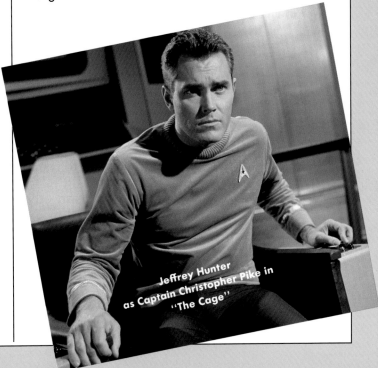

Jeffrey Hunter as Captain Christopher Pike in "The Cage"

Leonard Nimoy as Mr. Spock,
who is armed and ready for action
in front of the shuttlecraft *Galileo*

Creating a Legend

What does it take to create one of the most enduringly popular characters in science fiction? Luck, genius, or a bit of both?

As Leonard Nimoy says, "It is a combination of talents. Writing, directing, acting. But even with those elements present, there is no guarantee the magic will take place."

But take place it did, with the character of Spock. From the very beginning, Gene Roddenberry knew that he wanted an alien in his science-fiction series, and that he wanted Leonard Nimoy to portray that alien. Said Roddenberry, "I made [Spock] a half-caste, because I remember thinking a half-breed Indian would be a lot more interesting than a full-blooded Indian or white, because he's going to be tugged in many directions."

But the character's alien background had yet to be fleshed out. In the first pilot (and some of the earliest episodes), Spock can be clearly seen emoting. However, when the character Number One was discarded along with the first pilot, Spock took on her trait of non-emotion, and the magic began to happen.

"What immediately intrigued me," Nimoy says, "was that here was a character who had an internal conflict. This half-human, half-Vulcan being, struggling to maintain a Vulcan attitude, a Vulcan philosophical posture and Vulcan logic, opposing what was fighting him internally, which was human emotion. There was a dynamic there to work with from an acting point of view."

Nimoy was suddenly faced with a number of creative choices; how does one show that internal conflict if the character *doesn't* express emotion? In his book *I Am Not Spock,* he describes how the Genesis of Spock was influenced by singer Harry Belafonte's performance at Los Angeles's Greek Theatre during the 1950s:

"During the first forty-five minutes of [Belafonte's] program he stood perfectly still at a center stage microphone, his shoulders slightly hunched, his hands resting on the front of his thighs. He simply sang. Then in the middle of a phrase, he finally made a move. He simply raised his right arm slowly until it was parallel to the floor . . . Had he been moving constantly, the gesture would have meant nothing. But following that long period of containment it was as though a cannonball had been fired.

"I found this idea very useful in Spock. When a stone face lifts an eyebrow, something has happened."

After a time, Nimoy came to know the character intimately—so intimately, in fact, that it began to affect him personally. He says, "It was helpful in making me see things more precisely and dispassionately; to get an objective view of the situation. What I didn't realize was the pressure cooker it put me into because I was, in character, suppressing my emotions. Once I'd got [the Spock makeup] all on, it was the strangest thing. I saw it happening in the mirror. It was as though, if I fooled around or laughed a lot, my face would crack. As though I would damage myself in some way; destroy the character and hurt myself. So I would just sit around and the rest of the cast would be fooling around, telling jokes or whatever, and I would just sit there, impassive. I would be enjoying myself but I wouldn't express it."

Yet Nimoy's intimate knowledge of the character paid off, not only in his portrayal, but in other additions to STAR TREK lore. Certainly it was the reason the Spock neck pinch was created. The script "The Enemy Within" called for the Vulcan to steal up behind Kirk's evil alter ego and knock him out with the butt of a phaser.

Nimoy found the idea incompatible with Spock's pacifistic Vulcan philosophy, so he suggested to the director that Vulcans had studied human anatomy and developed a less violent method of rendering recalcitrant humans unconscious. The director asked for a demonstration. Nimoy "explained to Bill Shatner what I had in mind and when I applied the pressure at the proper point, Bill stiffened and dropped in a heap. That's how the Vulcan neck pinch was born."

Nimoy used his Jewish upbringing in creating the Vulcan hand salute, first used in the episode "Amok Time." The salute derived from that used by the Kohanim, Hebrew priests, when blessing the congregation while forming the letter *shin* with their hands. The gesture is now used as a greeting by STAR TREK fans everywhere.

Leonard Nimoy and Gene Roddenberry share a lighthearted moment on set of the first pilot

Kirk and the Captain's Yeoman (Andrea Dromm) on the bridge

everything *but* my career. Now, generally they ask you about some of the other things you've done, the other directors you've worked with . . . Apparently, Gene had done his homework and knew about that. So we just generally 'shot the breeze.' . . . Frankly, I walked out of the interview thinking I wasn't right for the part, and that's why he was carrying on the conversation in the way that he was."

It was also decided that the ship needed a chief engineer; the actor James Doohan was called in to read for the role. Roddenberry recalled, "Jimmy Doohan I had never worked with, but a director brought him in and asked him if he could do a Scottish accent and he did like an hour and a half of accents and had us falling on the floor laughing, so there was never any doubt that he had the job." Roddenberry asked Doohan which accent he preferred, and Doohan replied, "He's going to be an engineer so he should be a Scotsman." Doohan has always been fascinated by science and ships. Said he, "The writers of STAR TREK found out that I read technical journals. And that's how they put that into Scotty's character. The character is ninety-nine-percent James Doohan and one-percent accent."

With the cast in place, "Where No Man" was shot in July 1965 at a cost of $330,000. Filming took eight days, postproduction several months. Finally, in February 1966, word came from the network: STAR TREK would make its television debut in December.

There were changes after the second pilot as well. Roddenberry had always wanted to cast DeForest Kelley as the doctor, but Kelley had been busy doing other projects (including pilots for Gene). He remembers, "Gene had never discussed STAR TREK with me at the time except in the commissary one day before he started [production of the first pilot], and he said, 'De, I've got two properties . . .' I think he said for CBS at the time, and that one of them was a science-fiction thing called STAR TREK, and the other was 'High Noon.' Of course, I had been in a great number of Westerns. He said, 'Now, in the science-fiction story there's a very interesting character . . . He's an alien and he has pointed ears, and we're going to do him green.' I said, 'I'll wait for "High Noon."'"

In addition, NBC felt that audiences wouldn't buy Kelley in a "good guy" role, as he had played the role of villain too often (such as the despicable Amos True in *Gunfight at Comanche Creek*, who coolly silences a

The miracle worker, Montgomery Scott (James Doohan)

Making a Difference

As "STAR TREK" developed, Nichelle Nichols's frustration grew. While preliminary script drafts might show her character, Uhura, having a significant scene or two in the episode, final drafts invariably cut her contribution to "Hailing frequencies open, Captain." Finally, in desperation, she confronted Roddenberry, and when no satisfactory response came, she quit.

This occurred on a Friday. That night, Nichols chanced to attend an NAACP fund-raiser—and one of the attendees just happened to be Dr. Martin Luther King.

King, it turned out, was a fan of the show, and asked to be introduced to Nichols. When she confessed that she was leaving the series, King strongly urged her to remain, as her character served as a role model not only for blacks, but for everyone.

Because of his words, Nichols returned to the show, and later told Hugh Downs in a "20/20" interview, "I knew that now black children must look at me on that ship even if I was just pushing some buttons and know that 'this is a person I can identify with, that I can emulate.'"

One of those kids was Whoopi Goldberg, who told *Starlog* magazine, "I've been a Trekkie from way back. The only time you ever saw black people in the future was on STAR TREK."

Guinan and her role model: Whoopi Goldberg and Nichelle Nichols share a hug on the ST:TNG set

When Goldberg contacted the producers of ST:TNG and asked to be included in the series, they tried to politely decline. Gene Roddenberry assumed that a star of Goldberg's magnitude would insist on a leading role, but when he spoke with her, he learned otherwise.

"She said, 'No, you don't get it, do you? What I am saying is that I love STAR TREK. It's been close to my mind all my adult life and I want to play a part in the new series even if I just sweep the floor. I don't want to be the star of it. I don't want to deprive anyone of their job. I just want to be a part of what this is doing for people.' She had been affected by *The Original Series* and she understood, perhaps more than many, what drama could do for people."

Thus the character of Guinan, the hostess of Ten-Forward, was born, thanks at least in part to Nichols's decision to remain with *The Original Series*.

Mr. Spock and Lieutenant Uhura (Nichelle Nichols) take care of business on the bridge home. When Nichols went in to read for STAR TREK, there was no part in the script for her, so she read for the part of Spock. "We did a nice long reading, a scene that was several pages long," she recalls, "and when I finished, one of the guys said, 'Call down to personnel to see if Leonard Nimoy has signed his contract yet!'"

Grace Lee Whitney, who had appeared in the films *Top Banana* and *Some Like It Hot,* was hired to replace Andrea Dromm as the captain's yeoman. (Whitney had also appeared in Roddenberry's "Police Story" pilot with De Kelley.) Majel Barrett returned to the show in a different guise—that of Nurse Christine Chapel. NBC executives had not liked Barrett's portrayal of Number One, so Barrett came up with a plan: she bleached her hair blond and went into Roddenberry's office.

"I sat there talking to his secretary, Penny, and Gene walked in. He looked at me and at Penny, said, 'Good morning,' and walked in the door. . . . I kept on talking to Penny, and pretty soon Gene came out again, put some papers on Penny's desk, sort of smiled at me, turned around, and walked back in his office. Then the double take happened. He opened the door and said, 'Majel?!' And I said, 'By God, if I could fool you, I can fool NBC.'"

With characters in place, STAR TREK went into series production, at a cost to NBC of $180,000 per episode. By August of 1966, Roddenberry had settled into the role of executive producer, with Gene L. Coon as producer and Robert H. Justman as associate producer.

In September 1966, Roddenberry decided to garner a little advance publicity by showing the pilot "Where No Man" to attendees of the World

Kirk and ''Charlie X'' (Robert Walker, Jr.) prepare for a workout in the *Enterprise* gymnasium

Costumes by William Ware Theiss

So how in the puritanical 1960s, when a mere navel or the underside of a breast was enough to send network censors reeling, did STAR TREK's costume designer, the late Bill Theiss, manage to get away with so . . . little?

True, Theiss put *The Original Series'* crewwomen into ultra-short skirts well in advance of that decade's mini craze. And true, the female guest stars were clad in Theiss's beautiful—but undeniably alluring—creations.

Yet Theiss insisted that it was not necessarily the *amount* of skin shown that made the costumes seem extraordinarily revealing, but rather the manner in which that skin was shown. Hence the "Theiss Titillation Theory": The degree to which an outfit seems sexy is directly proportional to the degree it appears to be on the verge of slipping off.

Certainly, the theory applied to Leslie Parrish's pink chiffon Greek gown in "Who Mourns for Adonais?" It consisted of a fitted piece of chiffon that covered Leslie's bosom and was anchored solely at one point on the long, flowing skirt, and by the weight of fabric draped over one shoulder. Leslie reported that the costume was perfectly comfortable, and that she was not at all nervous about wearing it—while those around her reported exactly the opposite reaction.

The Titillation Theory had a corollary: Bareness in unexpected places. Said Theiss, "The costumes were designed to be bare in places that you normally weren't used to seeing bare skin. For the most part, they were not any more or less bare, or more or less structurally unsound. There were a few things that were very fragile, like in 'Elaan of Troyius,' that silver on black mesh thing that was constantly being sewed on the set because the mesh was so fragile. But that was done to utilize that particular fabric in that situation.

"I always tried to start out with what was appropriate for the script and the character . . . and what Gene liked." He always considered whether the clothing was suitable for the "planet of the week." And while in theory he designed for the future, he always kept in mind that the costumes also had to be acceptable to today's viewing audience.

When Roddenberry began putting together STAR TREK: THE NEXT GENERATION, he immediately recruited Theiss. In designing the new Starfleet uniforms, Theiss created another stir by putting a spin on the old miniskirt idea with the "scant," a short tunic worn by some of the *Enterprise*'s male

Costumer Bill Theiss adjusting one of his creations for Susan Oliver

crew members. The scant appeared mainly in first-season episodes.

A native of Boston, Theiss graduated from Stanford with a degree in design and landed a job as an artist in Universal's advertising department. From there, he moved on to CBS Television City, where he served as costumer for two soap operas. His television credits include "The Donna Reed Show," "The Dick Van Dyke Show," "My Favorite Martian," and "General Hospital," as well as two pilots for Gene Roddenberry—"Genesis II" and "Planet Earth." Theiss was nominated three times for an Oscar—*Bound for Glory* (1976), *Butch and Sundance: The Early Days* (1979), and *Heart Like a Wheel* (1983)—and won an Emmy for his costume designs on STAR TREK: THE NEXT GENERATION.

The Theiss Titillation Theory in Action: (Clockwise, from right) Lieutenant Carolyn Palamas (Leslie Parrish) and her seemingly precarious Greek gown in "Who Mourns for Adonais?"; Angelique Pettyjohn as drill thrall Shahna in "The Gamesters of Triskelion"; and Susan Oliver as the infamous green Orion slave woman

sign autographs, chaos ensued. Traffic was brought to a standstill, and Nimoy "escaped" only with the help of local police.

According to William Shatner's memoirs *Star Trek Memories*, Nimoy's escalating popularity began to bother Shatner, who freely admits that he was troubled by the realization that he was no longer the only star of the show. When Shatner voiced his concerns to Roddenberry, the producer responded, "Don't ever fear having good and popular people around you, because they can only enhance your own performance." Roddenberry discussed this problem in his correspondence with Isaac Asimov, who suggested that the close friendship between Kirk and Spock be emphasized on the show. That way, when viewers thought of Spock, they would naturally think of the captain as well. The advice worked.

Extremely rare photos of Shatner and Nimoy taken by photographer Ken Whitmore

Yet the STAR TREK characters' incredible popularity with their fans failed to be reflected in the Nielsen ratings. By the end of 1966, NBC let it be known that it was unhappy with the ratings—and considering canceling the show.

Science-fiction writer Harlan Ellison, who was then working on a STAR TREK episode, spearheaded the first "Save STAR TREK" letter-writing campaign. He sent out five thousand letters from "The Committee," a group of science-fiction notables that included Ellison, Robert Bloch, Theodore Sturgeon, Poul Anderson, Lester Del Rey, and Philip José Farmer. The letters urged series fans to write NBC protesting STAR TREK's cancellation.

Apparently, NBC was impressed with the response: the show was renewed for a second season. In the meantime, some of the finest first-season prize. . . . I rewrote that script for Harlan, and it won the Nebula Award, which he rushed up on stage and took credit for, too!"

At the beginning of the second season, a new character, Ensign Pavel Chekov, joined the *Enterprise* crew. According to the network's press release, Chekov was added because *Pravda* had complained about the fact that no Russians were represented on the show. However, actor Walter Koenig, who portrayed the young ensign, has a different take:

"Well, the facts are that they were looking for somebody who would appeal to the bubblegum set. They had somebody in mind like Davey Jones of 'The Monkees,' and originally it was supposed to be an English character . . . however, in acknowledgment of the Russians' contribution to space they made the decision to go that way."

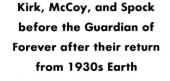

Kirk, McCoy, and Spock before the Guardian of Forever after their return from 1930s Earth

STAR TREK's "Other Gene"

The late Gene L. Coon joined the "Star Trek" staff in mid-first season to serve as writer-producer (a "hyphenate," in the TV industry parlance). The multitalented Coon had also freelanced for television shows like "Dragnet," "Bonanza," and "Wagon Train," as well as numerous others. He came to STAR TREK from a stint on "The Wild, Wild West" and later would go on to help create "The Munsters."

Coon brought welcome relief for Roddenberry, who was already exhausted from the strain of producing a weekly series. "By the time Gene Coon came on board," recalls original series producer Bob Justman, "Gene Roddenberry's physical stamina was about gone." Justman remembers Coon as speaking "in this odd, dry, clipped manner. He looked like a Methodist preacher from Arkansas"—in fact, Coon hailed from Nebraska. "Or a banker who's just about to foreclose on you. [When I first met him] I thought he was one cold, hard, mean son of a bitch. That was my physical impression of him. It didn't take long before I realized that Gene Coon, in addition to his enormous writing abilities, was a wonderfully warm, sensitive, generous, sweet, decent person. He was a phenomenon. I've seen people write before, but I've never seen anyone who could, when a script needed to be written, sit down in two days and not only knock out a script, but the script would be twenty or thirty pages too long. He was a machine gun. He was terrific."

Roddenberry agreed: "I found him to be an immensely inventive writer and immensely devoted to many of the things that I was devoted to. He had the ability to write fast and well. I remember once he did a forty-two-page memo on a thirty-eight-page script. We worked together on many things over the years. It was great fun. I loved him."

William Shatner notes that Gene Coon's arrival was soon followed by a noticeable improvement in later first-season scripts (among them "Devil in the Dark," "Errand of Mercy," and "Space Seed," all fully or partially credited to Coon).

The Prime Directive, the Organian Peace Treaty, and the series' favorite villains, the Klingons, all sprang from Coon's creative mind. He also had a talent for bringing characters to life; he helped develop the friendly feud between Dr. McCoy and Mr. Spock, and the characterization of Engineer Scott as a "complaining miracle worker."

Gene Coon at his typewriter

Coon's writing habits were as unique as his scripts. Every time he got mired down in a story problem, he simply went to sleep. By morning, when he woke, the solution always presented itself, and he would write at a frenetic—but never sloppy—pace until lunchtime, then take the rest of the day off.

During STAR TREK's three-year run, Coon also contributed to the episodes "Arena," "Metamorphosis," "Who Mourns for Adonais?," "The Apple," "Bread and Circuses," and "A Piece of the Action." He left as series producer during the second season to work on "The Name of the Game," though he wrote the third-year episode "Spectre of the Gun" under the pseudonym Lee Cronin.

Sadly, Coon died of lung cancer in 1973, before the series' "renaissance" and the advent of STAR TREK conventions; as a result, he was never interviewed as were others who worked on the show, and his great contribution to STAR TREK remains largely unsung.

Lieutenant Sulu (George Takei) at the helm, flanked by Ensign Pavel Chekov (Walter Koenig)

The Russian accent comes naturally to Koenig, whose father hailed from Lithuania and spoke Russian at home.

In the meantime, NBC had changed its mind about keeping Spock well in the background; because of the character's enormous popularity, the new network VP encouraged Roddenberry to focus more on the Vulcan. After all, it was becoming pretty clear that Spock's satanic good looks and Leonard Nimoy's ability to convey great depth of repressed emotion with the merest lift of an eyebrow struck a lot of female viewers as . . . well, sexy.

Said Nimoy, "The first indication [of Spock's sex appeal] was when a lovely actress visited the set with my agent. I was in costume with all the makeup on when we were introduced. She said, 'Oh, God, can I touch your ears?' It's a silly thing to say, I know, but she was serious. She really wanted to touch them."

It's no secret that most Vulcanophiles are women. Just what is the secret of Vulcan appeal?

"Something exciting about the devilish eyes and ears," Nimoy postulates. "A character who could not express emotions and, therefore, could not express love. That could express a challenge to a lady who believes she may be the one to teach him about love."

Whatever the secret, the Vulcans remain one of the most popular alien races in science-fiction history. As a consequence of growing interest in "Vulcanalia," the season's premiere was "Amok Time," which gave the viewing audience its first and only glimpse of Spock's home planet. Spock's already-established greater strength and keener hearing helped the STAR TREK staff work backward in establishing the planet's characteristics—greater gravity, thinner atmosphere. Writer Theodore Sturgeon certainly also understood about Vulcan sex appeal, for he introduced the *pon farr*, the Vulcan seven-year mating cycle. The episode also marked the first use of the Vulcan hand salute (which posed quite a challenge for guest actress Celia Lovsky, who played the matriarch T'Pau) and the now-famous greeting, "Live long and prosper."

All of Vulcan rolled into one package: The matriarch, T'Pau (Celia Lovsky)

T'Pring (Arlene Martel) stops a disgruntled Spock from ringing her chime

Another second-season "Vulcan" episode was "Journey to Babel," which introduced Spock's parents, the human Amanda and the Vulcan ambassador Sarek, and dealt with the eighteen-year rift between father and son. The episode was written by story editor D. C. (Dorothy) Fontana, one of the series' finest writers. Fontana's

scripts did much to develop the background of Spock, who she freely admits was her favorite STAR TREK character.

A veteran writer who had already sold nine television scripts, Fontana first came to work for STAR TREK in a secretarial position, but continued to freelance. During the show's first season, she wrote the episodes "Charlie X" and "Tomorrow Is Yesterday." Her talent so impressed Roddenberry that, near the end of the first season, as she recalls, "[he] called me and asked, '. . . Would you like to try [being] story editor?' And I said yes. He gave me a major rewrite to do. If I could do the rewrite on time and to the satisfaction of both the studio and the network, then I could be a story editor."

The rewrite was on Nathan Butler's [Jerry Sohl's pseudonym] script for "The Way of the Spores," which in Fontana's hands became "This Side of Paradise." According to Fontana, "The story started out being a love story for Sulu, and it really wasn't working. That's why Leila Kalomi was named as she

38

was. I'm sure that they assumed it would be someone like a Hawaiian-type girl. It just wasn't working because there were a lot of problems with it. I went in to Gene and said, 'You know what's wrong with this story? It should be a Spock love story.' And he thought about that for a while and said, 'Okay. Write that.' . . .

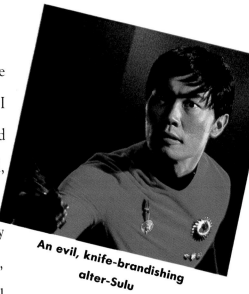
An evil, knife-brandishing alter-Sulu

"I had to do a complete and total rewrite . . . restructuring the story and changing the characters. Now it became Spock, and if Spock is affected, how does that change the relationships to the rest of the crew? If he can feel emotion, suddenly he's somebody they don't know. It was nice to have fun with it, because Leonard could sense the inherent ability to carry that off . . . now he's free, suddenly—he can do other things. And that was very liberating; that was fun."

Fontana went on to write some of the series' best episodes, including "Friday's Child," "By Any Other Name," "The Ultimate Computer," and "The *Enterprise* Incident."

In the middle of the second season, NBC again hinted that STAR TREK might be headed for cancellation. However, this time it wasn't a science-fiction writer who spearheaded the "Save STAR TREK" letter-

(*Below left*) Scott, McCoy, Kirk, and Uhura find themselves in a hostile alternate universe and midriff-revealing costumes in "Mirror, Mirror"
(*Below right*) A bearded alter-Spock invades McCoy's mind

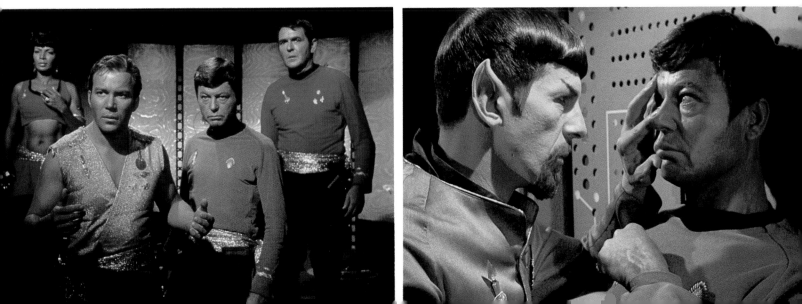

Social Consciousness

One of the advantages Gene Roddenberry had producing "STAR TREK" was that he was able to tackle social issues that would never get past the 1960s network censors on a more down-to-Earth drama. In the great tradition of Jonathan Swift and *Gulliver's Travels*, Roddenberry and the many writers who contributed to the "STAR TREK" universe were able to attain a level of social commentary that was ahead of its time—all because the series used the trappings of the fantastic as a backdrop. "STAR TREK" stories became morality plays, sophisticated enough to hold up and maintain their relevance nearly thirty years later.

"STAR TREK"'s special spin—born of the volatile era in which it was conceived—was that these morality tales could encourage viewers to think along the lines of such then-radical liberal beliefs as "All men are equal, no matter what the color of their skin" and "No good comes of getting involved in other people's internal wars."

This was strong stuff in the sixties. Only undisciplined youths and the occasional daring politician were bold enough to make such statements in public. Certainly no network with sponsors to worry about was going to put up with a mainstream television program taking these positions.

So "STAR TREK" used its science-fiction guise to make the statements more palatable. The most obvious challenge to the status quo was the racially mixed nature of the crew of the *U.S.S. Enterprise.* With forced busing a pressing concern, it wouldn't have been advisable to state openly, "Starfleet doesn't care if a person is black or white or yellow—this is an equal-opportunity employer." So "STAR TREK" openly stated that all *species,* like Vulcans, for example, were allowed to serve in Starfleet, while implying that the same held for all human races by casting a variety of minorities in visible roles.

It was "STAR TREK" that in 1967 aired the controversial interracial kiss between Captain Kirk and Lieutenant Uhura, the first ever on television. This was dangerous ground when there was a real danger that some affiliate stations, especially in the "Bible Belt," would "black out" or refuse to air the episode because of the kiss. In the end, no one warned the station managers about the episode's radical content and the episode aired across the country without trouble.

A love-smitten and happy Mr. Spock with Leila Kalomi (Jill Ireland) in "This Side of Paradise"

Racial tolerance was also the subject of an entire episode, "Let That Be Your Last Battlefield," which portrayed two eternally warring species, one black on the right side and white on the left side, the other black on the left side and white on the right side. The episode wasn't subtle in its approach, but it dealt with racial tensions and their potential tragic results in a way that no "real life" drama could have hoped to do.

Although Roddenberry had been a member of the U.S. Army Air Corps during World War II, he was never an advocate of military force. Both "A Private Little War" and "The Omega Glory" spoke out against Federation involvement in planetary civil disputes—again, a risky position to take when the country was in the midst of the Vietnam War.

While he promoted liberal thinking like peace and harmony, Roddenberry wasn't afraid to take on the counterculture by pointing out that drugs and a simple, carefree life were not the answer to society's

(*Above*) The infamous interracial
kiss scene

(*Right*) Kirk teaches the Hill
People to fire guns in the
Vietnam parable, "A Private
Little War"

ills. This was the case in both "The Way to Eden"
and "This Side of Paradise."

In "This Side of Paradise," Captain Kirk rejected
the simple, loving, commune-like lifestyle of the
colonists. For Kirk, the passive existence that was
caused by alien spores—a drug of sorts—went
against human nature. "Maybe we don't belong in
Paradise," Kirk says. "Maybe we can't stroll to the
music of lutes, Bones—we must march to the sound
of drums."

Once again, STAR TREK was ahead of its time in
pointing out the dangers of racism and intolerance
as well as the dangers of drugs and surrendering
one's individuality to a group consciousness.

Cheerful and efficient transportees Mr. Sulu, Lieutenant Uhura, Mr. Chekov, and Mr. Scott

filmed in September 1968. The episode made a bit of history by featuring television's first interracial kiss, between William Shatner and Nichelle Nichols. "They had originally written it with me teamed up with Spock for the first interracial kiss," remembers Nichols. "My understanding is Bill Shatner took one look at the scene and said, 'No you will not! If anyone's going to be part of the first interracial kiss in television history, it's going to be me!' So they rewrote it."

The scene made the network executives extremely nervous; fearing that Southern affiliates might refuse to broadcast the episode, they asked the actors to shoot the scene two ways: one in which the kiss actually occurred, one in which it didn't. Nichols quips, "So because Bill and I are such staunch perfectionists and respect our craft and our profession, we did not balk at thirty-six takes!"

According to her, the only fan mail that protested came from "one guy who said, 'I'm a white Southerner, I believe in the separation of the races, but any time that a red-blooded American boy like Captain Kirk gets a beautiful gal like Lieutenant Uhura into his arms, he ain't going to fight it.' That was the big, major protest."

Unfortunately, STAR TREK could not survive its difficult Friday-night time slot. In February 1969, NBC announced that the show would be canceled. Ironically, "Turnabout Intruder," the final episode, was aired less

44

than six weeks before humans first set foot on the moon.

William Shatner reports that he felt great sadness, and a sense of anxiety about the future. For him, he says, "STAR TREK went out not with a bang but with a whimper, a cold sweat, and a stomach ache."

"We knew it was the graveyard slot," said DeForest Kelley. "We knew it was on its way out. We felt all along that we were doing something rather special, that this was a show that should not go off the air."

"I had mixed emotions," said Leonard Nimoy. "I felt tired and drained. It had become a battle to maintain the quality of the show. . . . You hate to see anything good die, but on the other hand, you hate to see anything good piddle its way into mediocrity or worse."

But STAR TREK was far from dead . . . as the fans soon proved.

Part Two

STAR TREK®

THE IN-BETWEEN YEARS

Kirk finds himself in a magical universe where technology fails to function in "The Magicks of Megas-tu"

provided input by writing the episode "The Infinite Vulcan." Many of the cast read for more than their original roles; James Doohan, who read the part of Scotty, often supplied several other voices. In the episode "Yesteryear," for example, he provided the voices of the Andorian, the Healer, and the Guardian of Forever.

Fontana solicited several writers from The Original Series to provide scripts for the animated show, and not a one turned her down. Samuel A. Peeples, Stephen Kandel, David Gerrold, Margaret Armen, and others (including Fontana herself with "Yesteryear") contributed episodes. Actor DeForest Kelley commented, ". . . most of the scripts were not written for children. They are adult scripts and some of them are very good, and would have made good [live-action] STAR TREK's."

Reviewers concurred. The *Los Angeles Times* said:

NBC's new animated STAR TREK is as out of place in the Saturday morning kiddie ghetto as a Mercedes in a soapbox derby.

Don't be put off by the fact it's now a cartoon. . . . It is fascinating fare, written, produced and executed with all the imaginative skill, the intellectual flare and the literary level that made Gene Roddenberry's famous old science fiction epic the most avidly followed program in TV history, particularly in high IQ circles.

NBC might do well to consider moving it into prime time at mid-season . . .

Certainly one of the finest episodes of the animated show was "Yesteryear," the only one written by Dorothy Fontana; her production responsibilities allowed no time for writing. She recalls, "It took three months to complete one episode from start to finish, and that's rushing. This was due to all of the handwork involved—the hand painting. The only thing that they could do fast was when you had duplicate cells, they could Xerox them. And they didn't have color Xeroxes then, so they all had to be hand painted."

Part Three

STAR TREK®

THE FILMS

It all started when Paramount acquired the STAR TREK copyright from Desilu in the late 1960s, and decided to present the "property" as a syndication package. There were plenty of takers; in fact, the show became a hands-down hit in syndication.

By 1975, Roddenberry and Paramount were having serious talks about STAR TREK II. But the project soon evolved from TV series to a modest-budget $3 million movie.

Roddenberry immediately set to work on a first draft of the screenplay, and soon turned in "The God Thing," a story about a computer with damaged programming and delusions of godhood. It also contained some elements that readers will recognize: a transporter accident that scrambles bodies, and a scene that shows Spock as a postulant with the Vulcan Masters.

Paramount rejected Roddenberry's effort, but was determined to come up with a suitable script. Soon, a steady stream of writers were making their way onto—and off—the Paramount lot. In February 1976, writer Harlan Ellison jokingly told interviewer Tom Snyder, "There have been nine hundred and sixty-seven writers called in on this project. Last word, there was no script. They've got a director, they've got a start date. No script. I think they're going to stand there and whistle. Who knows?"

Finally, the writing team of Chris Bryant and Alan Scott came up with a story idea that Paramount liked, which involved the ancient Titans (who turn out to be our friends aboard the *Enterprise*, thanks to the magic of time

Mr. Spock tries to contact V'Ger in STAR TREK: THE MOTION PICTURE

travel). However, the script itself was actually written "by committee"; by the time everyone had had a turn rewriting Bryant and Scott's original draft, the story line that had been approved was unrecognizable. Paramount wound up rejecting that effort.

By late 1978, the discouraged executives finally decided that, since no one was coming up with a "big enough" idea, perhaps STAR TREK was really best suited for television after all. Paramount executives started talking about a fourth network—with a brand-new live-action STAR TREK series as its cornerstone. Robert Goodwin and Harold Livingston were brought in to produce the new series, and writer Jon Povill was hired as associate producer and story editor. Most of the original cast returned—with the notable exception of Leonard Nimoy, who was not available at the time. In his place, David Gautreaux was cast as the Vulcan science officer Xon, and a new actress, Persis Khambatta, was cast as the navigator Ilia.

With several scripts purchased, actors hired, and the series ready to go, Paramount had a sudden change of heart. Less than three weeks before production was to begin, Paramount executives pulled the plug on the new series. Why?

Well, for one thing, plans for the fourth network fell through. But the most compelling reason can be neatly summed up in two little words: *Star Wars.*

Awed by *Star Wars*'s financial success at the box office, Paramount suddenly realized that it had a potentially very lucrative property on its hands: STAR TREK, which would no longer be a modest television series, but a theatrical special-effects extravaganza. And so STAR TREK, which

Spock and Scott get technical

Lieutenant Xon ''Star Trek II's Lost Vulcan''

As STAR TREK II entered preproduction, all *The Original Series'* actors were signed to reprise their roles, except for Leonard Nimoy. Needing a Spock replacement to fill a similar slot in the new stories to be told, Roddenberry developed Lieutenant Xon (Pronounced ''Zahn'') as the *Enterprise's* Vulcan science officer. Intriguingly, Xon is clearly a character in the best tradition of some of STAR TREK's most popular characters: Spock, Data, and Odo.

The Writer's/Director's Guide for STAR TREK II begins its character description of Xon by asking, ''Can a twenty-two-year-old Vulcan on his first space voyage fill the shoes of the legendary Mr. Spock?'' This constant comparison of Xon with Spock was to be part of Xon's ongoing struggle to fit into the predominantly human environment of the *Enterprise.*

And, like the android Data, he would encounter many of the same frustrations and challenges. As the Guide goes on to say, ''Xon will be engaged in a constant struggle within himself to release his buried emotions to be more human-like for the sake of doing a good job . . . we'll get humor out of Xon trying to simulate laughter, anger, fear, and other human feelings.''

When the STAR TREK II television series became STAR TREK: THE MOTION PICTURE, Nimoy was finally signed to reprise his role as Spock. David Gautreaux, the actor who was cast as Xon, eventually appeared in the film as Commander Branch of the Epsilon 9 communications station destroyed by V'Ger.

The Vulcan that never was: David Gautreaux in full Vulcan regalia as Xon

Lieutenant Ilia ''My celibacy oath is on record''

*B*ecause she was a completely new character, and not a replacement, the Deltan navigator, Lieutenant Ilia, survived the transition from STAR TREK II, the series, to STAR TREK: THE MOTION PICTURE. The main difference in her role in the television script and the film version was that for television, since she was to be a regular character, she was restored to life by V'Ger at the end of the episode.

Like Xon's similiarity to other STAR TREK characters, Ilia shares a certain similarity to *The Next Generation*'s Deanna Troi—specifically, Troi's limited sensing ability. In the STAR TREK II Writer's Guide, Ilia is described as having ''the esper abilities common on her planet . . . the ability to sense images in other minds. Never words or emotions, only images . . . shapes, sizes, textures.''

However, Ilia's most notable characteristic was almost the complete opposite of Xon's. Where Xon had to struggle to overcome his repressed emotions,

Ilia had to struggle to keep one specific kind of emotion repressed. As the Guide explains, ''On 114-Delta V, almost everything in life is sex-oriented . . . it is simply the normal way to relate with others there. Since constant sex is not the pattern of humans and others aboard this starship, Ilia has totally repressed this emotion drive and social pattern.''

Again echoing *The Next Generation*, Ilia and Commander Will Decker, Kirk's second-in-command, share a relationship similar to that of Deanna Troi and Will Riker. Both couples had a romance in the past, which they try to put behind them now that they serve on the same starship.

Though Persis Khambatta auditioned for the role of Ilia in a bald cap, as did all the other actors trying for the part, when actual production on STAR TREK: THE MOTION PICTURE began, she did shave her scalp completely.

The refitted *U.S.S. Enterprise* NCC-1701

had come so close to being resurrected as a television series, then a low-budget movie, then a series once more, was finally destined to become a major motion picture.

On March 28, 1978, Paramount held a press conference to announce that STAR TREK would soon become a $10 million movie. All the original cast, including Leonard Nimoy, had been signed and were in attendance that day. When asked whether he would find it difficult to play Captain Kirk after nine years away from the role, actor William Shatner replied, "I think Spencer Tracy said it best—'You take a deep breath and say the words.' Of course you have to have some years of experience to know how to say the words and suck in your breath. An actor brings to a role not only the concept of the character but his own basic personality, things that he is, and both Leonard and myself have changed over the years, to a degree at any rate, and we will bring that degree of change inadvertently to the role we re-create."

Leonard Nimoy had signed his contract barely twenty-four hours before, and at the time of the press conference, his character had yet to be written into the script. When asked why he had been so reluctant to play Spock once more, he stated, "It's really not a matter of reluctance. We had a lot of details to iron out. There have been periods of time when the STAR TREK concept was moving forward and I was not available. . . . When the project turned around and I was available again we started talking immediately. It has been complicated, it has been time-consuming. But there was never a question of reluctance to be involved in STAR TREK on my part. I've always felt totally comfortable about being identified with STAR TREK and being identified with the Spock character. It has exploded my life in a very positive way."

Veteran director Robert Wise (*West Side Story, The Sound of Music, The Day the Earth Stood Still*) was also present at the press conference, and said, "Science fiction is something that's always interested and intrigued me, but I've never had a chance to do this kind of show. I think it can make an absolutely fascinating picture. I'm looking forward to my involvement with all the cast and the marvelous special photographic effects that we can bring to it. I'm very excited."

But although the actors and directors had been signed, no script yet existed. It was finally chosen from the scrapped STAR TREK II series' pilot, "In Thy Image." Harold Livingston wrote the teleplay based on Alan Dean Foster's treatment; the teleplay was soon expanded by Livingston (with help from Roddenberry) into a screenplay.

Paramount spent an enormous sum on the film's special effects, first hiring Robert Abel and Associates, then Douglas Trumbull. The cost (which

**The *U.S.S. Enterprise*
approaches space station
Regula I**

Paramount rejected that effort as well—right about the same time that they signed a gentleman by the name of Harve Bennett to a development deal. Bennett had served as a producer for CBS Television, then as vice-president of programming for ABC; he went on to become producer of "The Mod Squad" and executive producer of "The Six Million Dollar Man" and "The Bionic Woman."

Bennett remembers, "A week after I arrived there, they called me in to see Messrs. Bluhdorn and Diller and Eisner and Katzenberg, and to a lesser extent, the man who had brought me there, Gary Nardino, who was Head of Television at Paramount.

"It was a total surprise to me. Rather quickly, Bluhdorn got right to it and said, 'Can you make a STAR TREK II for a television-type budget? For less than forty-five million dollars?' I said, 'Where I come from, I could make four or five movies for that.' Which was prophetic."

Bennett said the following of his role in STAR TREK: "Credit for the success of the show, of course, goes to Gene Roddenberry. There's no disputing his genius. But it also goes to Gene Coon, the hardheaded rewriter who made a lot of things work.

"I think of myself, sometimes, as the Gene Coon of the feature movies. Fandom never understood the contribution made, notwithstanding Roddenberry's genius."

Bennett had never before watched an episode of the original STAR TREK; he immediately sat down and watched all seventy-nine episodes. His homework paid off; he became intrigued by the character of Khan Noonian Singh in "Space Seed," and soon came up with a story that dealt with Khan's

"Remember"

Scott and McCoy struggle to hold Kirk back from trying to save his dying friend

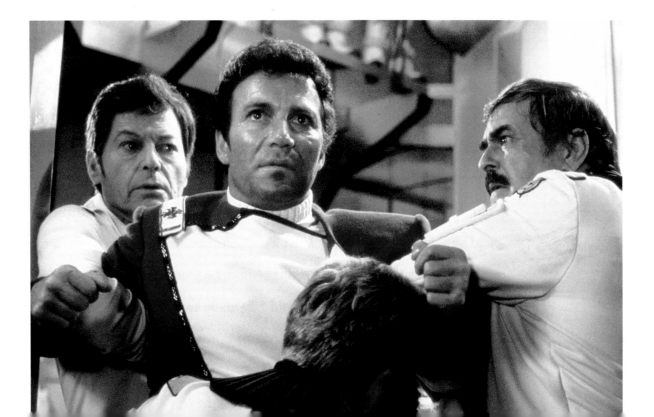

Our heroes land a Klingon Bird-of-Prey on the planet Vulcan

play to in STAR TREK. You have to play up those elements that are universal to human beings."

This time, the movie focused more on action, adventure, and the deep-felt camaraderie that had first made STAR TREK so popular. Critic Janet Maslin of *The New York Times* summed up its reception best: "STAR TREK II—Now that's more like it." *The Hollywood Reporter* called the film "far superior to its predecessor."

Once again, Paramount had another hit on its hands—and once again was eager to make a sequel. But would the movie have to be made without one of STAR TREK's most popular characters?

Maybe not. By the time Spock's death scene was filmed, Leonard Nimoy was beginning to have second thoughts. "I wasn't excited about not

Enter Harve Bennett

A multiple-choice question: What is the *Kobayashi Maru?*

    A. A third-class neutronic fuel carrier, carrying a crew of 81 and 300 passengers, last heard from in the vicinity of Sector Ten.
    B. The toughest test that cadets face in their years at Starfleet Academy.
    C. The brilliant solution to a very difficult public-relations problem.
    D. All of the above.

When Harve Bennett, executive producer of STAR TREK II: THE WRATH OF KHAN, asked Jack Sowards, author of the film's screenplay and cowriter of the story along with Bennett, to come up with a simulator test that had no solution, he had more than a great opening scene in mind.

"What I had designed," says Bennett, "was that the picture would open—and the audience would think we're in space, we're in a desperate situation, and it's very realistic, and all of a sudden, when they think the ship's going to blow up, a screen rises and James T. Kirk walks through the smoke and says, 'Well, you screwed that up.'"

Bennett smiles at the recollection. "If you think it was just sheer genius that I should decide to start a movie that way, it wasn't. I'm a pragmatist, a responsive player. What preceded the scene was the fact that word was out about my *first* idea for the film."

Bennett recalls that Leonard Nimoy had been reticent about reprising his role as Spock in the second STAR TREK motion picture. In early talks with Bennett, however, the actor had allowed that if the producer came up with a good story, he'd reconsider. And Bennett had done it. "I said, 'Leonard, you must be in this movie because we're going to kill you, and there'll be no more burden of putting the ears on.'"

Nimoy was intrigued. "He said, 'How will you kill me?' 'Just like Janet Leigh in the movie *Psycho*,' I told him. 'We're going to kill you one-third of the way into the movie, where they least expect it, and you're going to die heroically. And the rest of the movie will be, Let's get the bastards who killed Spock.' He said, 'I love it, it's wonderful, I'll sign.'"

But while the film was in preproduction, word leaked out about Spock's impending death, and all hell broke loose in fandom. "The world was screaming, 'You're going to kill Spock!' So I called Leonard and I said, 'Leonard, we're really screwed.

Admiral Bob, played by Harve Bennett in his cameo role from STAR TREK V: THE FINAL FRONTIER

We can't kill you now because everybody knows we're going to kill you like Janet Leigh.'"

However, Bennett soon realized that he might be able to use the public's knowledge to his advantage. "So I told Leonard, 'Okay, I promise, you're still going to die, but now you have to die at the *finish* of the movie.'" Nimoy agreed to the change, and Bennett set to work on "throwing tinfoil into the radar of those who knew," deliberately leaking rumors and half-truths about alternate endings being shot. The strategy worked; the filmmakers couldn't restore surprise, but they could establish ambiguity.

A similar technique was used in the film itself. Since the fans were expecting Spock to die in the beginning, á la *Psycho*, Bennett and Sowards fulfilled their expectations by killing Spock in the simulator during the first fifteen minutes of screen time. "It was a way of saying, 'Aha, just kidding, folks,' and knowing people would say, 'Oh, they weren't really going to kill him—they were just pulling our legs.' And then, when he died at the end, it caught them totally unawares!"

**Director Leonard Nimoy
as his alter ego, Spock**

When the producers of STAR TREK III: THE SEARCH FOR SPOCK called Leonard Nimoy to ask whether he would like to be involved with the project, Nimoy's immediate response was ''You're damned right, I want to direct that picture!''

Nimoy's interest in directing was nothing new; as early as 1965, he audited the directors on ''The Man from U.N.C.L.E.'', which means that he was given access to the set and allowed to carefully observe the directors. In 1972, he directed an episode of ''Night Gallery''; in 1982, an episode of ''Powers of Matthew Star''; in 1983, an episode of ''T. J. Hooker.''

How did cast members react to having their former coworker directing them? According to William Shatner, ''We were brothers in flesh and spirit. And now, suddenly, my brother was saying, 'You should do this,' and I would say, 'I think I should do that.' . . . It was more awkward in the beginning than any of the other films, but that slowly erased itself as I realized that Leonard had a point of view and knew what he was doing.''

Fellow actor James Doohan reports, ''[Nimoy] comes to the set with his homework done, the cinematographer's homework done, and if you allow him to, he would show you that he has your homework done, too. He's really terrific.''

Nimoy the actor appeared only at the conclusion of STAR TREK III—and a good thing, too, he says, for he found self-direction extraordinarily challenging.

''The biggest problem I had, and this is really silly, but it happens that it was the scene in the sickbay of the Bird-of-Prey. Spock is unconscious and McCoy is talking to him. Now, not only am I in the scene, but I have to play the scene with my eyes closed. So I can't even look to see if the actor I am playing the scene with is looking anything like I think he should look. It drove De Kelley crazy. He swears that I was trying to direct him with the movement and flutter of my eyelids. It was very difficult. In a sense I was very pleased and relieved that the design of the story allowed me to do a minimal amount of performing.''

Sizing himself up as a director, Nimoy allows, ''I'm probably somewhere in between Bob Wise and Nicholas Meyer. Not as precise as Bob, not as imaginative or rough-edged as Nick. I think the major difference, and for me the most important difference, is my attitude toward the story and the actors. They [Wise and Meyer] are looking for a different kind of final product than I am.''

STAR TREK III: THE SEARCH FOR SPOCK was a hit. Nimoy was subsequently offered the directorial reins for STAR TREK IV, which—to date—remains the most popular of the STAR TREK films. After its release, Nimoy became a much-sought-after director. He went on to direct the 1987 hit *Three Men and a Baby* as well as the critically acclaimed film *The Good Mother* (1988).

But despite the lack of utter surprises, the picture was a rousing success. Reviewers were uniformly enthusiastic. According to the *Los Angeles Times,* "For all its spectacle in space, its humanity once again outweighs its hardware, and its innocence is downright endearing." Said *USA Today:*

Leonard Nimoy boasted years ago he could direct a better STAR TREK movie than the first two because he has a better sense of what made the TV series a hit. And he was right. STAR TREK III: THE SEARCH FOR SPOCK is the best *Star Trek* movie of the three, and the closest to the original spirit created by producer

Directed by Nicholas Meyer

Nick Meyer is not just a director, but a writer of renown whose novels include *The Seven Per Cent Solution, The West End Horror,* and *Black Orchid.* He also penned the screenplay *Time After Time* (based on Karl Alexander's novel *The Time Travelers)* and went on to direct the popular film. Meyer also adapted his own book *The Seven Per Cent Solution* into a script, for which he received a 1978 Oscar nomination; he has also received two Emmy nominations—one for cowriting *The Night That Panicked America,* and one for directing the television movie *The Day After.*

Interestingly, before he was asked to direct STAR TREK II: THE WRATH OF KHAN, Meyer had never seen an episode of STAR TREK. However, he didn't view that as a hurdle. "There are only two kinds of art," he said, ". . . good and bad. The only allegiance to the content of STAR TREK that I felt I owed was to that which struck me as good. I felt that I owed *no* allegiance to anything that was bad, for any reason whatever. My feeling, when I was working on [STAR TREK II] was to divide things up with that in mind. I didn't like the costumes from any other version, so I made new costumes. I didn't like the sets, so we reworked the sets. If I didn't like the dialogue, I reworked the dialogue."

In approaching STAR TREK II, Meyer decided that he wanted to give the film an "adventure on the high seas" feel:

"I said I'd really like to stretch the nautical analogy. I said it should be like Captain Horatio Hornblower in outer space. I made everyone on the set watch the movie version of Hornblower. The young midshipman who gets killed . . . he's stolen right out of that movie. And it was interesting, because when I first spoke to Bill Shatner about my idea, he said, 'That's interesting; that was also Gene Roddenberry's original take on it.' So far, so good. But I really wanted to pursue it. I had ship's bells, and botswain's whistles and all that sort of stuff. And we very much stressed the idea of the ships as galleons in space . . . And the other thing I kept saying: Because I'm not very interested in science fiction but I *am* interested in stories about people, the only reason for me to make this movie is if they can be real. Why can't they do things that we do now? I hate when they say 'negative' when they mean 'no.'"

The "high seas" theme continued in STAR TREK VI: THE UNDISCOVERED COUNTRY, which Meyer wanted to have a claustrophobic, gripping *The Hunt*

Nick Meyer directing the action in STAR TREK VI

for Red October feel. (The phrase "the undiscovered country,") taken from *Hamlet,* refers to death. Meyer had originally used it as the subtitle for STAR TREK II; it was changed at the last minute by an executive. "And it just so happens," Meyer says, "that in slightly different context, the name is as applicable to STAR TREK VI as it was for STAR TREK II."

Meyer's films tend to include a generous sprinkling of literary allusions—from *A Tale of Two Cities* and Milton in STII, and Shakespeare in STVI. (He co-wrote the screenplay for STAR TREK IV and cowrote the screenplay for STAR TREK VI with Denny Martin Flinn, based on a story he cowrote with Leonard Nimoy and Flinn.) Says he, "I think I also make movies primarily for people who read. It doesn't mean that only people who read can get off on them, but the more you read the more you're going to get off on the little touches of that type that are in there."

Commenting on his career as a writer and director, Meyer mused, "I'm the most fortunate person I know. I realize it every day of my life. There's not a day that I don't walk onto a set and say, 'Oh my God, I can't believe I'm doing this!'"

succeed in winning peace between the Federation and the Klingon Empire. This idea became the touchstone for the film's dramatic tension.

In the end, Nimoy acted as executive producer of STAR TREK VI and Nicholas Meyer directed from a script he co-wrote with Denny Martin Flinn.

In the production, there was a sense, from the very beginning, that this would very likely prove the final film with all of the original cast. Said William Shatner of the experience of acting in STAR TREK VI, "It was a very pleasant experience filled with nostalgia even in the act of making it, realizing that this was the last and that I would probably not work with these

The accused listen to the Klingon translation of courtroom proceedings in STAR TREK VI: THE UNDISCOVERED COUNTRY

97

Part Four

Photography by Gary Hutzel

STAR TREK depicted us in reckless youth, with a Starship captain who tamed space as vigorously as we laid claim to the future . . . STAR TREK: THE NEXT GENERATION reveals the child grown—a little more polished, but also more complacent. And if there's a bit of gray and a wrinkle or two, so much the better.

—Gary D. Christenson, TV Guide, July 23, 1988

It began in 1986, when Paramount executives couldn't help noticing that they had a string of hit STAR TREK movies on their hands. If STAR TREK could successfully make the transition to film, why couldn't another television series do just as well? With, say, an all new cast, so that salaries wouldn't be prohibitively expensive, and so that the original actors could continue making movies without interruption. And if the new show caught on, well, then someday there could be movies with *that* cast, and then maybe . . .

Paramount soon offered Gene Roddenberry creative control of the project. It was decided that, unlike the aborted STAR TREK II, this series would not be a thinly disguised rehash of *The Original Series*, but a brand-new look at the STAR TREK universe some seventy-eight years in the

future. Instead of a "space Western" with shoot-outs between the bad guys

and our heroes, the new show would favor a pacifistic, intellectual approach

to solving problems. Nor would there again be the dominant triad of captain,

doctor, Vulcan science officer; instead, the emphasis would be on a "family"

of characters, giving the show a more "ensemble" feel. As Roddenberry said,

"I don't think we need a retread crew with people playing the same kinds of

roles. I'm not at all sure we'll have a retread Vulcan. I would hate to think

our imagination is so slender that there aren't other possibilities to think

about."

As fate—or luck—would have it, all four networks (including Fox)

turned down the new STAR TREK, which actually suited Roddenberry, who remembered his battles with NBC censors, just fine. Paramount made the decision to syndicate the new show, which meant that instead of being carried by individual television stations who were part the group of stations that made up a network, STAR TREK would be sold to individual stations in each market.

With a budget of over $1 million, Roddenberry went about the task of gathering his creative team. He immediately hired STAR TREK veteran Robert Justman, who recalls: "I wanted to work with Gene again. We worked very well together and we always had a good time. And I wanted to do the show even better than it had been done in the past. The concept of going back to work again on it and making it better seduced me. I went back to work for one season, after which I retired, having accomplished my objective."

Writer David Gerrold, of "The Trouble with Tribbles" fame, and producer Eddie Milkis were also called in. The quartet brainstormed, eventually producing a writer's bible containing input from everyone. Dorothy Fontana was soon brought on board to write the two-hour pilot, and Robert Lewin became writing producer. Artists were hired to provide twenty-fourth-century designs. Andrew Probert set to work on designing the new *Enterprise* (NCC-1701-D); Rick Sternbach updated the STAR TREK props and equipment, while Michael Okuda (whose graphics are now fondly referred to by cast and crew as "Okudagrams") provided a new look for the show's graphics and computers. Bill Theiss, who had created costumes for *The Original Series,* was called in, and George Lucas's Industrial Light and Magic was hired to provide the initial special-effects shots. Academy

Befriending the enemy: Picard addresses the young Borg known as Hugh in ''I, Borg''

Picard consults his old Academy mentor Boothby (Ray Walston) in ''The First Duty''

Casting the Captain, Part II

The first casting decision for STAR TREK: THE NEXT GENERATION was made in an extraordinary way by veteran STAR TREK producer Robert Justman.

One evening, Justman and his wife happened to attend a UCLA lecture series that featured British actor Patrick Stewart. The moment Stewart began to speak, Justman excitedly told his wife, "I think we've just found our captain." As Justman later reported, "once I saw him, that was the captain in my mind. I just couldn't shake it. I've never been so sure of anything as I was with that."

But Roddenberry, who wanted a French actor in the role, failed to share Justman's certainty. In fact, he suggested that the Englishman would be better cast as Data. "I got Patrick Stewart's picture and I looked at it, astonished," Roddenberry recalled. "And I said, 'I'm not going to have a bald Englishman for a captain.' Almost everybody had that reaction. But then I became aware of Stewart's acting ability. And I saw him in a lot of things. The more I saw him, the better I liked him."

Says Justman, "We couldn't find anyone who would satisfy Gene—or ourselves, really—who was good enough. And finally at the end Gene relented and said, 'Well, let's go with Patrick. He's our best choice.' "

The studio shared Roddenberry's hesitancy. Stewart was called back several times, but no commitment was made, so he returned to England. "[Their interest] was not something that I took seriously for one moment," he says. "For every thirty interviews you go for, one of them might turn into an offer. I had no expectations whatsoever." But Stewart was soon summoned back to Hollywood to read for the part again. "And they just said, 'Thank you again,' and I left."

And then Stewart was called back *again*. This time when he arrived in Hollywood, he learned that he was to read wearing a hairpiece. This was Friday evening; Stewart was due to read first thing Monday.

Says he, "I discovered there are things that you can do if you try hard enough. Sunday morning, my wife drove my hairpiece—he's known as 'George,' this hairpiece—to Heathrow, and put it in an envelope into somebody's hand who took it on the plane and took it off. And that afternoon I drove to a little shed somewhere out in the fringes of the Los Angeles airport and picked up George. I remember thinking, 'My God, they better offer me this job after what it's cost me!' "

"The minute we looked at [the toupee], we realized it was wrong," said Gene Roddenberry.

Captain Jean-Luc Picard
(Patrick Stewart)

"That wasn't the Patrick we wanted. He looked like a drapery clerk."

So George's cross-Atlantic journey was in vain; fortunately, Stewart's wasn't. He landed the job. "I absolutely didn't expect it at all. Not remotely. I just laughed about the whole thing. Thought it was ridiculous. When I came over to do the pilot show, I didn't unpack my suitcase for a whole month. I had a conviction that one morning they would all simultaneously wake up and say, 'What have we done? We have cast this middle-aged, bald, Shakespearean actor as the captain of the *Enterprise*. We must have been insane!' "

Before the decision to cast Stewart was finalized, another actor by the name of Stephen Macht was being considered for the role of Picard. Dorothy Fontana remembers, "Stephen had played the captain in the film *Galaxina*, a comedy. He's an excellent actor with a craggy face who projects real strength, real masculinity. They called Stephen back [to read for the part of Picard] three times."

Had Macht been cast in the role, says Fontana, "he would have played a very different captain—more American, more direct. And his name probably wouldn't have been Picard!"

Fans who want to see what the *Enterprise*'s captain might have looked like can check out the STAR TREK: DEEP SPACE NINE episodes "The Circle" and "The Siege," in which Macht plays General Krim, a Bajoran military officer.

felt about the audition that, Well, there it is, I've done it. It's now behind me and I've done my best. So I spent a long time . . . over a long leisurely breakfast while my agent and other people were scouring the town looking for me to tell me I got the role. Then, I think, was the most difficult period of thinking hard about the job and thinking about whether it was something I should do."

It wasn't until after he began playing Picard that the full impact of his decision hit home.

"I didn't know . . . that what I was getting involved in was so subtly, deeply, profoundly interwoven into American culture. . . . I didn't know that I was sailing into history with this. . . . For a long time, people would say to me, 'Oh, you're the next William Shatner'—a phrase that used to irritate me at times. Now I see it in its proper perspective. . . . You know, all those original actors have practically become legends."

The next major role cast was that of the *Enterprise*'s first officer, William T. Riker. The producers had difficulty making up their minds in that case, as well.

Jonathan Frakes, who finally landed the role, remembers: "It was a long and winding road. I auditioned seven times over six weeks. I've often said it was harder getting the job than it is doing it. But I was lucky . . . [Roddenberry] took me under his wing after about the fourth audition." Frakes had won supporting roles in the miniseries "North and South," as well as "Falcon Crest" and "Paper Dolls." Prior to STAR TREK, he had just come

Riker in Mintakan garb in "Who Watches the Watchers?"

producers that they called him back to guest star as the Traveler in two ST:TNG episodes.) Soon Spiner was being slathered with makeup for screen tests. "I was every color under the sun," he says. "It was unbelievable! I was bubble-gum pink, I was steel gray, I was chartreuse—I was everything! They decided on gold contacts for me finally. I actually see clear through them because the pupils are clear. I also had every kind of wig you could possibly imagine before we settled on my own hair."

Spiner had appeared in several Broadway musicals and in the Woody Allen film *Stardust Memories*; perhaps the role of his best known to television viewers is that of a down-on-his-luck hick on the sitcom "Night Court."

Troi goes undercover as a Romulan in "Face of the Enemy"

Interestingly, British actress Marina Sirtis auditioned not for the part of Counselor Troi, but for Security Chief Hernandez. Bob Justman remembers, "Gene and I saw the movie *Aliens* together. And in [the movie] there was this female with whom Gene was much intrigued. She was a very feisty marine and she played a Latina. She was quite good. [Our character's] name was going to be Macha Hernandez."

But Sirtis brought a warmth and empathy to the reading that the producers decided would work very nicely in the role of Troi. However, had they made the decision to offer her the part one day later, she would have been back in England. As she explains, "The actual day that I was offered the job I was packing to leave. I had been in Los Angeles for six months. I started auditioning for STAR TREK in the middle of March, and at the beginning of May I was due to go back to England because my visa had run out . . . But I had gone out the day before and had bought my family and

Of the audition, he says, "I had come to the point in my life where I was ready for anything. So I went there [to the ST:TNG producers' offices] and gave it my best shot. I had a problem at first understanding the role of a blind officer. I tried to act blind while auditioning. The producers took me aside and told me about the VISOR device which allows Geordi to see like anyone else. Then I read the dialogue again with this in mind and apparently they liked the job I did."

Burton also quips, "When the show first started, Geordi was the pilot. It was this great line joke: Here's this blind guy flying the ship . . ."

Actress Gates McFadden, who plays Dr. Beverly Crusher, came with an extensive background in live theater and also as a director-choreographer whose credits include Jim Henson's *Labyrinth* and the fantasy sequences in *Dreamchild*. McFadden reports with a smile that she had a very different idea of Beverly Crusher when she first read for the role. "I thought this was the

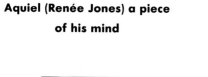

Geordi gives his beloved Aquiel (Renée Jones) a piece of his mind

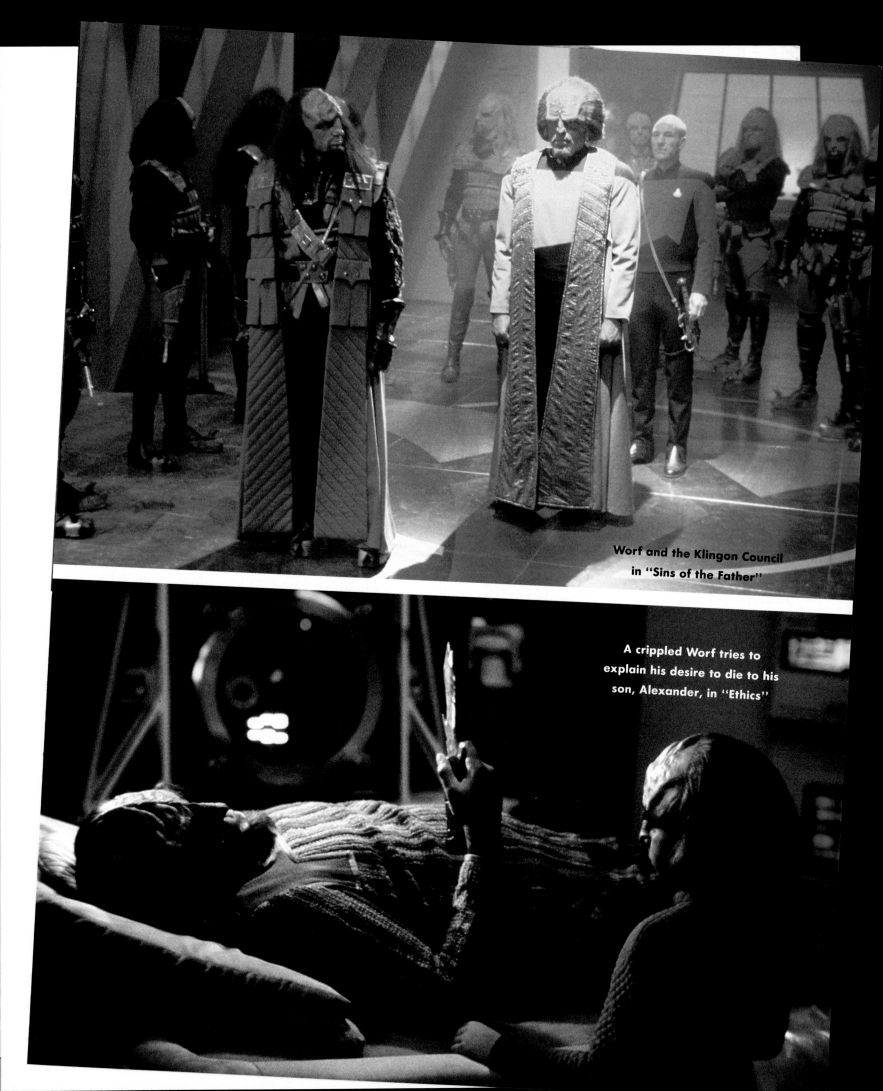

Worf and the Klingon Council in "Sins of the Father"

A crippled Worf tries to explain his desire to die to his son, Alexander, in "Ethics"

Q (John DeLancie) takes a
look at what makes Data tick
in "Deja Q"

The *Enterprise* crew acts out a
Q-generated Robin Hood
scenario in "QPid"

and read the scene and I said, 'Dorothy, I just don't know whether or not I can do this. I have a feeling that this show should be *their* show entirely and I don't know whether an intrusion by me would be appropriate or not.' But I did tell her that I thought it was a beautiful moment and that I liked it very much. . . . So then Gene called me and we had lunch together and he expressed his desire for me to do it, too. And I began to think about how much Gene has meant to me . . . I thought it would be . . . a way for me to say thanks for all that he had done for me over the years."

Included in the pilot was Irish actor Colm Meaney, who would go on to become series regular Miles O'Brien on both ST:TNG and *Deep Space Nine*. Meaney read for a part in the new series, but failed to land it; even so, his work won him a background part on the *Enterprise* bridge.

The pilot episode began filming in June 1987. The week of September 28, independent stations began broadcasting the premiere.

Humanity on trial in "Encounter at Farpoint"

"Relics" — Rebuilding the Bridge

"I really wanted to do the holodeck sequence for 'Relics' on the old bridge," explains Ronald D. Moore, coproducer of STAR TREK: THE NEXT GENERATION and writer of the popular episode. "I sold them on the idea conceptually, but it was a money question. It would be an expensive set to re-create and we weren't going to be able to do it if it cost too much."

Moore asked Michael Okuda, scenic-art supervisor and technical consultant for *The Next Generation*, about the feasibility of re-creating the bridge. A longtime fan of *The Original Series*, Okuda loved the idea, but recognized its difficulty. It was, however, "one of those ideas that ignited everybody's imagination," he recalls.

In researching the project, Okuda's boss, production designer Richard James, soon discovered that there were no accurately scaled drawings of the original set available. Nevertheless, James says, "we started looking at the series and plotting size, trying to get a scope of how big the set was, and how much of it we would need to build." When the initial estimated budget came in too high, James had a brainstorm. "If we could find an episode of *The Original Series* where it has an empty bridge, we could use that as a blue screen process, and then I'd just build a pie-shaped wedge for the live action to be shot against." This, he pointed out to the producers, would be much less expensive, and when Dan Curry, *The Next Generation*'s visual-effects producer, came up with an appropriate shot from the episode "This Side of Paradise," the project was green-lighted by the producers.

Additional cost cutting was achieved when Mike Okuda managed to track down Steve Horch, another avid fan of *The Original Series*. "Steve is a very good model maker, and he had built Chekov and Sulu's console and the captain's chair for use at conventions," says Okuda. "He was kind enough to loan it to us."

James incorporated Horch's pieces into the set, the heart of which was Scotty's engineering station, which also had to serve as the console on the opposite side of the room. "The director, Alex Singer, did a remarkable job of generating different coverage by cheating and using different angles on that one wall," notes Okuda. "Richard James had the clever idea of constructing alternate inserts of the upper panel above Scotty's station, so we could actually change the one screen to two screens when we were pretending it was the opposite direction."

Other contributions were made by set decorator Jim Mees, who found the bases of some classic sixties-style Knoll chairs similar to those that had been used on the bridge, and modified the top portions to match the originals. And professional model maker Greg Jein provided the production with the original buttons that had been used on the consoles. The buttons had been part of a collection of *Original Series* flotsam and jetsam that Jein had picked up from a retired effects man who'd worked on the show.

Incorporating the film footage from "This Side of Paradise" was an equally inspired task. "We got the briefest snippet of this long shot of the bridge from the episode—literally, just a few seconds," says David Takemura, visual-effects coordinator for "Relics." "So

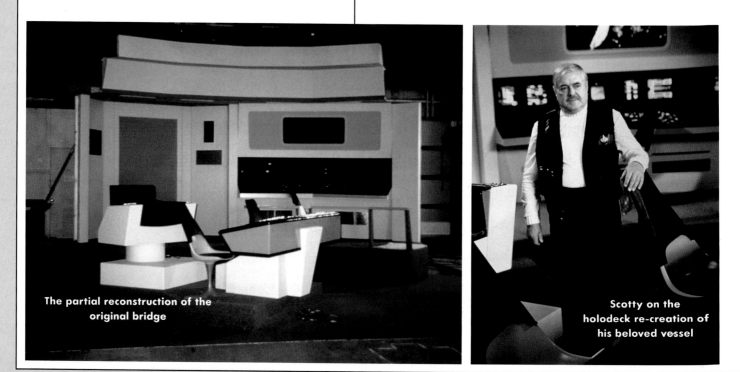

The partial reconstruction of the original bridge

Scotty on the holodeck re-creation of his beloved vessel

we transferred that interpositive to the medium that we work in, digital tape. And we had to cycle that two seconds and print it over and over again to make that background plate long enough for the shot when Scotty walks into the holodeck, which is about a ten-second shot."

"The first shot that we see through the holodeck doors is the scene from 'This Side of Paradise' that is blue-screened in through the holodeck doors," explains Mike Okuda. "The next cut that we see is that same wideshot of the bridge, with Jimmy Doohan blue-screened as if he's walking in the set—an over-the-shoulder shot. Dan Curry and [visual-effects supervisor] David Stipes reviewed the old footage, along with the director of photography Jonathan West. They figured out what kind of lens had been used for the original episode, the camera height, the positions of the lights, so they were able to accurately photograph Jimmy in such a way that he photographically fit into the set."

As difficult as the episode was for all involved, there was a real sense of accomplishment and a sense of carrying on a tradition. "Working on that bridge gave us a real appreciation for the artists that had worked on the original STAR TREK," says Okuda. "We very painstakingly tried to re-create everything, even the 'blinky light' patterns on the consoles, as accurately as possible. And when the special-effects staff fired up the blinkies, the sense of 'this is what it must have felt like to stand on that original bridge' was quite remarkable."

"Relics" — Writing the Story

"I've always had a love of classic STAR TREK and a love of those characters and of that series," says Ronald D. Moore, coproducer of The Next Generation and writer of "Relics." "It brought me to this show and gave me the job that I have now, so I really wanted to do 'Relics.' It was a privilege to finally give a little something back to something that was very influential in my life."

But how did the idea behind this little gem come about? According to Moore, the saga of "Relics" began when a writer named Michael Rupert submitted a premise to the producers. "He pitched a story where we come across a craft and a man is held in stasis by using the transporter beam," recalls Moore. "We thought that was a neat idea, but we didn't like the story that went along with it. And chatting around the idea of the technical gimmick, [executive producer] Michael Piller came up with the idea of using it as a device to bring back one of The Original Series characters. He suggested Scotty."

After buying the premise from Rupert, Moore was asked to write a story about bringing Scotty to the U.S.S. Enterprise using the transporter gag. "Scotty was a good choice because he's a fun character," says Moore. "He allows you a certain amount of freedom that I think we missed when we had Spock [in the fifth-season two-parter "Unification"]. Spock is a wonderful character, very complex, and yet you could have a little more fun with Scotty . . . he's a joker, he's a little broader, and there was a sense that this could be a lighter episode and be a lot more fun."

Moore's script for the show is full of loving tributes to The Original Series, from Scotty's reminiscences of the Dohlman of Elaas and the "wee bit of trouble" he encountered on his first visit to Argelius (references to

Actor James Doohan with writer Ronald D. Moore

Scotty prepares to raise his glass in a poignant toast to the original Enterprise crew

the episodes "Elaan of Troyius" and "Wolf in the Fold") to Data's comment "It is green," regarding the mystery beverage in Ten-Forward (drawn from Scotty's own comment to an inebriated Kelvan in "By Any Other Name").

But the show's writing had resonance that reached beyond STAR TREK's loyal corps of fans. Episode director Alex Singer recalls that when his wife, "who has no connection to the past of the show," visited the set during the filming of the holodeck sequence, she was moved to tears by Jimmy Doohan's performance as Scotty. And Singer himself had a similar reaction. "I cannot but be moved when Scotty salutes the invisible crew that's not there. I'm not what you'd call a Trekkie, but I sure know what that gesture means. I've lost enough friends and enough of my past that it's a universal gesture. The story was very moving to me."

Ro Laren (Michelle Forbes) looks into the face of her past in "Ensign Ro"

showing that we were just as capable of behaving evilly ourselves. Ensign Ro, a recurring character played by the talented Michelle Forbes, was introduced for reasons explained by Rick Berman: "The other characters in the cast are relatively homogenous; some might even say bland. So we wanted a character with the strength and dignity of a Starfleet officer but with a troubled past, an edge." The "edge" in this case was the fact that the temperamental, headstrong Ro had been court-martialed—and later pardoned—for disobeying orders, an act that led to eight deaths. The Bajoran Ro immediately became popular with the fans, and the story of her people's conflict with the Cardassians would soon form the basis for a new series . . . called STAR TREK: DEEP SPACE NINE.

All Good Things . . .

Only rarely in the history of television does the last episode of a show attract nationwide attention—most shows go out with a whimper, not a bang. Until 1994, only "The Fugitive" and "M*A*S*H" had so touched the hearts of the viewers that their passings were considered a cultural event. Then, in 1994, STAR TREK: THE NEXT GENERATION came to the end of its TV existence, and that ending became an event watched not only by America, but by the world.

Fans everywhere looked on as a chapter in the STAR TREK saga came to a close. The show that had been so much a part of so many people's weekly lives was leaving the air for good. True, it was going on to bigger and better things—STAR TREK: GENERATIONS, the first STAR TREK movie to feature the *Next Generation* cast. Even so, ST: TNG's absence from the small screen was something that was keenly felt, especially by those who worked on the show. "The last day of filming was very emotional for the cast and crew," said Lolita Fatjo, script coordinator for *The Next Generation*. "The behind-the-scenes support staff all stopped what they were doing and went down to the set to be a part of the final moments of what we all felt to have been one of the greatest times in our lives."

The Next Generation certainly left on a high note, with one of the program's most sweeping and powerful episodes, one that reaches all the way back to the show's beginnings. Seven years ago, Captain Jean-Luc Picard first faced the judgment of the Q Continuum—a race of being with godlike powers over time and space who presumed to gauge humanity's fitness to exist in the galaxy. Seven years ago they suspended judgment, but now their decision has been reached: The human race will be eliminated, not only in the present, but throughout time. Humanity will have never existed.

Picard, of course, finds a way to save the human race, and in the process learns more about himself, the finale being not so much an ending as a beginning. His experience leaves Picard and his crew even better prepared to face their future on the silver screen and whatever challenges may await them out where no one has gone before. . . .

This court is now adjourned: Q as judge in "All Good Things . . ."

Part Five

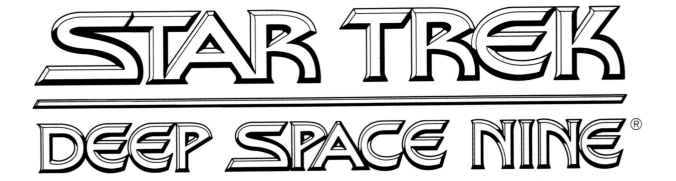

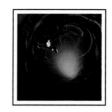

S hortly before Gene Roddenberry's death, in late 1991, Paramount executive Brandon Tartikoff asked Rick Berman to create a new, replacement series for STAR TREK: THE NEXT GENERATION, suggesting that it might be, rather than a "Wagon Train to the Stars," a "Rifleman" in space.

"Do you want to do another science-fiction show or another science-fiction show that is based on STAR TREK?" Berman asked.

"That's up to you," replied Tartikoff.

It just so happened that Berman and Michael Piller had been kicking around ideas for a replacement series—some STAR TREK–based, some not. Berman immediately contacted Piller and the two began brainstorming, ultimately deciding to go with the TREK-based idea.

Says Piller, "If it weren't STAR TREK, we still could have done it, but . . . When it became STAR TREK, it was a real blessing because we could use all of the texture, history, aliens, the entire universe that Gene created. We knew it well and we knew how to make it work, and that allowed us to do several things."

Since the new show would premiere while STAR TREK: THE NEXT GENERATION was still on the air, the pair decided against having a show featuring a crew aboard a starship. And, says Michael Piller, "If you're going to have a show set in space, you basically have three options—on a ship, on an alien planet, or on a space station."

Berman explains, "We had a lot of concerns regarding making a show that was going to be different but not different, making a show that was going to remedy some of the things that were problems on *The Next Generation* but

**Deep Space Nine
in all its glory**

However, there can be no denying that *Deep Space Nine* has returned to *The Original Series'* "Western" model, with more action and adventure (and a "Dodge City" of a space station). Another difference between *Deep Space Nine* and *The Next Generation:* characters are now allowed to have interpersonal conflicts (something Roddenberry had nixed in *The Next Generation,* insisting that people would be too mature for petty conflict by the twenty-fourth century). According to Brandon Tartikoff's "Rifleman" suggestion, the commander, Benjamin Sisko, would be a single father—faced by the problems not only of unresolved grief and parenting a child alone, but by the massive rebuilding of a devastated planet and space station. And he would often find himself at odds with his second-in-command, a Bajoran national. From the start, Berman and Piller had hoped that that Bajoran would be Ensign Ro, who had appeared in STAR TREK: THE NEXT GENERATION.

Berman recalls, "Before we really started developing the story, we knew that we wanted Michelle Forbes to be part of the show as a Bajoran female. She's an actress we are very fond of and very impressed with. Michelle had just signed a deal to do a feature film and decided she didn't want to commit herself to a series . . . But all this was really before the characters were developed. It's not like we took Major Kira and plugged her into a spot that had been held by Ensign Ro. Basically, once we knew that Michelle wasn't going to be joining us, we sat down and developed our story, and one of the characters that was created was Major Kira."

The creative duo also knew they wanted a character who would serve as a "mirror" of the human condition—an outsider, an alien.

A woman not to be trifled with: Nana Visitor as Kira Nerys

How Far We've Come

*F*rom its inception, STAR TREK made a strong commitment to what is now called multiculturalism—a commitment to the idea that by the time humanity spreads outward into space, conflicts based on such trivial things as gender, skin color, and place of origin will be an artifact of the past. It was no accident that STAR TREK presented television's first interracial kiss: it was part and parcel of the basic philosophy of the show.

STAR TREK: DEEP SPACE NINE continues and amplifies this tradition. That the station is commanded by a black man, that his first and second officers are women, that the station doctor is of Middle Eastern descent—these facts are worthy of notice in our society but not in the society inhabited by the characters on the show. To them, this is completely normal: Why shouldn't it be like this? How else would humans behave? This is a smooth continuation of the commitment to forging a better future that has always made STAR TREK unique among American dramatic television series.

Nowhere is this more evident than in the *Deep Space Nine* episode "The Forsaken," when Commander Benjamin Sisko inquires how Dr. Bashir is coping with the assignment he's given him—that of showing a group of obnoxious VIPs around the station. The commander and the doctor have a simple, amusing conversation about the travails of such duties, and how Sisko managed to get his superiors to give that kind of burdensome assignment to someone else. There's nothing unusual about this conversation—it's the kind that goes on every day in offices all over the world. The difference is that when a black man is talking to a Middle Eastern man in a typical television drama, they are almost certain to be talking about drugs, crime, terrorism, or violence—and are most likely to be presented as uneducated, heavily accented, immoral, or antisocial—but never on STAR TREK, where no matter what a character's ethnic background, conversations center around basic human interactions; where educated, articulate professionals of all kinds and colors work together smoothly in pursuit of noble goals; where the color of someone's skin, black or white, blue or orange, says nothing about the content of their character.

It is always far more effective to demonstrate something than to just talk about it, so rather than merely tell us that we *should* all get along, *Deep Space Nine*, following the grand STAR TREK tradition, shows us that we can get along, and that we will—and that we will all be the better for it.

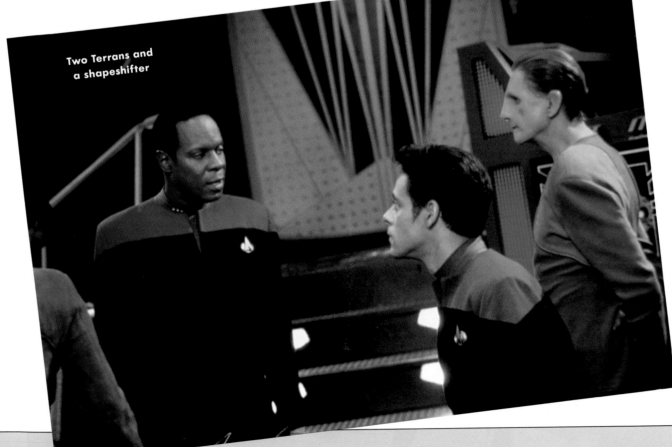

Two Terrans and a shapeshifter

"It's a dream come true to be a part of this," Shimerman enthuses. "It's a dream come true that I can beam up, that I can be part of the legend that I watched as a child, that I revisited when *The Next Generation* came on. Those shows were history long before *Deep Space Nine* was even created. Now I'm a part of all that."

The part of Odo went quickly to veteran actor Rene Auberjonois, probably best known to television viewers as Clayton on the series "Benson." He has also appeared in the films *M*A*S*H*, *The Eyes of Laura Mars*, and *The Ballad of Little Joe*, and had a cameo in STAR TREK VI: THE

Quark and the Ferengi female Bel in "Rules of Acquisition"

UNDISCOVERED COUNTRY as the assassin, Colonel West. "I'm not actually in [STAR TREK VI], technically speaking," Auberjonois admits. "Nicholas Meyer is a friend and he called months before they started it. He said, 'It would be a hoot if you came and did a day's work on it.' . . . I did it as a lark, because Nick is a friend." Auberjonois thought his part had been cut (it had, in the theatrical release) until a STAR TREK convention audience informed him that it had been reinstated in the video version.

He was delighted to get the part of Odo, and says, "My experience with television has always been that the first season takes time to really get going. There is a lot of shakedown, kinks that need to be worked out. With *Deep Space Nine*, I've been astonished at the quality of the scripts from the first

Odo and his mentor, scientist Dr. Mora (James Sloyan), in "The Alternate"

A mirror-universe Sisko makes Kira squirm in "Crossover"

She credits Marina Sirtis with helping to set the stage for *Deep Space Nine*'s stronger female characters. "It's very possible that Marina's lobbying and outspokenness about it has benefited the women in *Deep Space Nine*. I was attracted to the script right away by the strength of my character. Actually, both Kira and Dax are powerful women. To play a strong woman on television, or in any medium, really, is unusual, very rare, and it's a huge joy for me."

She had no reservations about committing herself to a possibly long-running series, for as she says, "This is not just an acting job for me. I have a wonderful character to play and I'll be able to play Kira for a long while. I'm not worried about a long run, to tell you the truth. It's a really tough time out there, especially in our business. To be working is great. . . . I'm just thrilled and grateful to be working, and to be working on STAR TREK."

At the suggestion of *Deep Space Nine* films, Visitor exclaims, "Wouldn't that be something? STAR TREK is already a huge part of my life and it always will be. . . . Every role changes you. . . . Every role I've ever done, there has always been a little ghost of it that stayed with me, and I know Kira will, too. I like Kira."

Siddig El Fadil, fairly unknown to American television audiences when he was cast as the young doctor, got the role in an interesting way. Born in the Sudan to British parents of Indian ancestry, El Fadil returned with his family to England shortly after his birth. He soon developed an interest in acting, and got his first break in "Big Battalions," a British miniseries. Soon thereafter, he appeared as King Faisel in "A Dangerous Man, Lawrence After Arabia." Unbeknownst to him, that performance won him the *Deep Space Nine* role. He explains, "['A Dangerous Man'] played here on PBS and I think it was one of the lowest-rated PBS shows ever, but that's the one that Rick Berman saw me in, thank God. Rick's probably one of the few people who saw it. That's what made him think of me for *Deep Space Nine*. So, I can thank that film and its great lighting and direction for me being here now. I'm just glad Rick saw it."

To accommodate El Fadil's background, the young doctor's surname was changed from Amoros to Bashir.

El Fadil recalls with amusement the fact that he once told his agent he wasn't interested in doing series television— unless, of course, he could get a

Sisko relives an idyllic picnic with his late wife, Jennifer, in "Emissary"

"It was definitely overwhelming in the beginning," says Farrell of her role, "but now I'm getting the hang of it all. . . . As an actress, I just try to look to the oldest, most mature part of myself when I play her [Dax]. They also gave me a tape of 'The Host' [the ST:TNG episode that introduced the Trill race], which I watched several times."

Born in Iowa, Farrell began her career as a fashion model. She appeared on the covers of *Vogue, Mademoiselle,* and many other fashion magazines while she studied acting. She got a costarring role on "Paper Dolls" (on which she worked with Jonathan Frakes). Her other television experience includes guest-starring appearances on "Family Ties," "The Cosby Show," "The Twilight Zone," and "Quantum Leap." Her film credits include *Back to School* and *Hellraiser III.*

"I was so freaked out when I got the part," she admits. "I was so overwhelmed. It was like, 'Oh, my God! This show is the second spin-off of a legend I watched when I was a kid.' It's really a living legend."

Once the cast was finally assembled, the production team went into overdrive during the filming of the pilot, which aired in late January 1993. The two-hour premiere episode of *Deep Space Nine*, "Emissary," received stellar ratings and solid reviews, demonstrating that viewers were hungrier than ever for new STAR TREK stories. And "Emissary" provided all the action and adventure an audience could hope for—plus a character study of Sisko, still tormented by unresolved grief over his wife's violent death.

Lwaxana Troi (Majel Barrett) expresses interest in Odo's unique physiology

Kira dons a Vedek's robes in "The Siege"

"The Circle": Kira at Vedek Bareil's temple

The combination of character development plus action marked *Deep Space Nine*'s first season. As Rick Berman says, "The first seven shows are very character-based, internal-type shows that explore . . . the community of the space station." Indeed, the very next episode ("A Man Alone") focused on Odo's character. Soon after came an examination of Kira's past and a test of her current loyalties ("Past Prologue"), and the episode "Captive Pursuit," which focused on Miles O'Brien and his friendship with an alien. Also included in that first seven was "Dax," by STAR TREK veteran D. C. Fontana. The first season was also marked by visitors from *The Next Generation*: Q, Vash, and Lwaxana Troi (who lusts after the abashed Odo).

"As the year went on," notes Berman, "we began to feel a little claustrophobic about that [the focus on the space station and its characters] and, for the next group of episodes, we really spread our wings and showed what this franchise was capable of doing. Finally, we ended with some . . . issue-oriented episodes [such as "In the Hands of the Prophets," which took on religious fundamentalism] that showed we could do traditional STAR TREK storytelling."

The following season opened with a bang and a twist—a three-part adventure consisting of the episodes "The Homecoming," "The Circle," and "The Siege," all of which deal with Bajor on the verge of revolution, and Kira's loss of (and return to) her *Deep Space Nine* post. Romance featured prominently in many episodes, with love affairs for Bashir, Quark, and Sisko. The second year also featured the notable return of the original STAR TREK's favorite Klingons—Kor (John Colicos), Kang (Michael Ansara), and Koloth (William Campbell) in the compelling "Blood Oath."

Vedek Winn (Louise Fletcher) and Minister Jaro plot to take control of Bajor and oust the Federation

O'Brien helps rescue Bajorans from a Cardassian prison in ''The Homecoming''

Back in Action

Among the fiercest foes Captain James T. Kirk ever faced were the Klingon officers Kor ("Errand of Mercy"), Kang ("Day of the Dove"), and Koloth ("The Trouble with Tribbles"). Despite the passage of time, these three alien soldiers, played respectively by John Colicos, Michael Ansara, and William Campbell, had never been forgotten by the viewers of STAR TREK. So it was with great excitement that STAR TREK fans everywhere received the news that the three best-known *Original Series* Klingons would be returning to STAR TREK in the STAR TREK: DEEP SPACE NINE episode "Blood Oath."

Now in their declining years, Kor, Kang, and Koloth meet on *Deep Space Nine* to plan one last military campaign, this time of a most personal nature: they have at last located the hidden fortress of the Albino, the renegade Klingon who decades earlier murdered the three warriors' firstborn sons. They have come to *Deep Space Nine* to take on the last member of their party, Jadzia Dax, who, in her previous life as Curzon Dax, had sworn a blood oath to avenge Kang's child, who was Dax's godson and namesake.

The idea of using the old Klingon characters in this episode came up in a conversation between

Deep Space Nine producer Peter Allan Fields, co-executive producer Ira Steven Behr, and executive producer Michael Piller. "We were quite pleased that all three of these fine actors were willing to reprise their roles," said Fields, who wrote the script for the episode. The return of Kang, Kor, and Koloth was moving and powerful, as these well-known characters go on what turns out to be their final adventure.

This episode provided *Deep Space Nine* with what up to that point was its strongest connection to its roots, weaving it tightly into the universe created in *The Original Series* that is the fundamental underpinning of all things STAR TREK.

Those working on "Blood Oath" felt this special connection being made. Mike Okuda, scenic art supervisor for *Deep Space Nine* said, "At first, you almost didn't recognize them because they were in heavy Klingon makeup. But as soon as Michael Ansara opened his mouth, there was a powerful sense of déjà vu. Having the three *original* Klingons on the show was magical for everyone."

Kor (John Colicos)

Koloth (William Campbell)

Kang (Michael Ansara)

Three grand old warriors on a final mission of honor

Of course, no mention of *Deep Space Nine*'s second season would be complete without the two-part episode "The Maquis," which introduced a new group of Federation outlaws—some of them former Starfleet officers— who protest the effects of a Cardassian-Federation treaty. The Maquis, of course, went on to figure prominently in a television show called STAR TREK: VOYAGER.

The episode "Crossover" (teleplay by Peter Allan Fields and Michael Piller, story by Peter Fields) borrowed an intriguing concept from *The Original Series*: that of the alternative universe in "Mirror, Mirror." "Crossover" shows what became of the treacherous mirror universe some eighty years after Kirk and company visited it. When Kira and Bashir take

Old friends at odds: Starfleet officer-turned-terrorist Cal Hudson (Bernie Casey) and Ben Sisko in ''The Maquis, Part II''

The Defiant is boarded, and Major Kira is seized by a Jem'Hadar soldier in "The Search"

a "wrong turn" in the Wormhole, they find things have changed. The station Deep Space Nine is once again referred to as Terok Nor, ruled by Intendant Kira Nerys under the watchful eye of the Klingon-Cardassian Alliance. In this harsher reality, Terrans provide slave labor, Odo is the slave driver, and Sisko is a pirate. This time, instead of the Mirror-Spock being convinced to help our "real" heroes, Mirror-Sisko listens to Kira's impassioned plea and has a change of heart.

The final episode of the second year, "The Jem'Hadar" (written by Ira Steven Behr), introduced the ferocious storm troops of the Dominion, the mysterious power that controls much of the Gamma quadrant. The season ended on a note of anxious anticipation: The Dominion was out there, ready and waiting to invade. But was the station ready for them?

THE DEFIANT

The *Defiant* was originally built as a warship designed to fight the Borg. It's fast, heavily shielded, and bristling with weapons. The design of the Bridge reflects its mission—most of the consoles are devoted to weapons and tactical systems, and everything is centered around a single command chair. No first officer or ship's counselor here—this was designed to be the hot seat, from which the captain would oversee the fight against the Borg. The ship's interior is spare and functional; there are no luxuries, in fact crew members often have to share quarters: small rooms with two bunks each. The ship has minimal scientific facilities, can carry a complement of about fifty people, and has a top speed of warp 9.8

—*From the revised STAR TREK: DEEP SPACE NINE bible, 8/1/94*

Finalized design sketches

We knew at the end of second season that the story lines were going in a direction that required a larger ship, with armament and much more warp-speed capability, and the ability to hold a larger crew," recalls production designer Herman Zimmerman of the motivation to create a new vessel for STAR TREK: DEEP SPACE NINE's third season. "The *Defiant* was a big boost for the show's bag of tricks."

The introduction of the *Defiant* opened the door to a variety of action-packed story lines that could feature more members of the crew than one of DS9's trusty little runabouts. "We had always intended to do a lot of stories off the station by using the runabout," explains coproducer Robert Hewitt Wolfe, "but it just wasn't working as a set. It was too small to do multicharacter scenes, and awkward for staging conversations and action. You can't do a fight scene in the cockpit of a runabout—not very easily."

Designing *Defiant* was something of a process of elimination. "One of the marching orders was, 'It

can't look like *Voyager*,' and it can't look like the bridge of the *Enterprise*-D. *Defiant* needs to be wonderful but not competitive," states Zimmerman. "So I conceived the bridge as being more linear, with more depth. *The Original Series*'s *Enterprise* was built on a circular floor plan. *The Next Generation*'s *Enterprise*-D was built on an oval floor plan, as was the bridge of *Voyager*, which was built on the same sound stage as THE NEXT GENERATION bridge. The *Defiant*'s bridge has a rectangular floor plan."

"With the initial construction of a bridge, a corridor, and some quarters, it became a lot easier to go off the station, and have adventures," Wolfe notes. "Unlike the sets for the runabouts, the sets on the *Defiant* are easy to shoot. Their size makes it possible to have a number of people in a scene."

During the third season, Zimmerman supervised construction of a number of sets: the ship's engineering area, a mess hall, and some additional corridors. The fourth season would see the construction of a new Jefferies tube. "We'd been sharing the Jefferies tube with *Voyager*, which is actually the same one that they'd used for quite a while on THE NEXT GENERATION," Zimmerman notes. "But we feel we're in a position now where the two shows need to look different. And they need their own stuff, in case there's a conflict over physical space or time."

From a story viewpoint, the producers' primary hope is that the relatively spacious surroundings of *Defiant* will convey a similar sense of the breadth of the Gamma quadrant. "We've opened up the ability to go off the station, something we obviously needed to do," says Wolfe, "not just to establish the 'bad guys' in the Gamma quadrant, but just the Gamma quadrant as a whole—to make it a place with a real sense of depth where we need to spend some time."

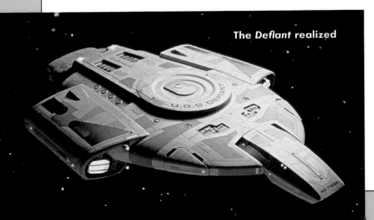

The *Defiant* realized

roots, getting into the Dominion and the Founders." The group came upon an intriguing idea: What if the Founders were actually shapeshifters —Odo's long-lost relatives? But they were hesitant, thinking that Michael Piller would never approve the concept.

One day, Piller showed up for lunch. And, according to Behr, he said, "'Look, I have this cockamamie idea—you'll probably hate it and laugh me out of here, but—what if the Founders turn out to be shapeshifters, Odo's people?' We all just cracked up."

As for introducing the warship *Defiant*, Behr says, "Some say that we brought on the *Defiant* because we wanted to become more like *The Next Generation* or *Voyager*. The truth is, once we created the Dominion, the Founders, and the Jem'Hadar and realized that this space station was the *only* thing standing between them and the Alpha quadrant—well, Robert Wolfe and I realized we needed another ship, a kickass ship. It was

In a parallel universe, Sisko has the chance to save the Mirror-Universe version of his wife, Jennifer (Felecia M. Bell), in "Through the Looking Glass"

The Poster on the Edge of Forever

When Captain Kirk and Mr. Spock leaped into Earth's 1930's in STAR TREK: *The Original Series* episode "The City on the Edge of Forever," sharp-eyed fans may have spotted a rather nondescript advertising flyer. Posted on a brick wall in an alley, it promoted a boxing match. Such items of set decoration are standard in film and television production; they function to establish time periods or geographical and social areas without resorting to boring expository dialogue. In this case, the boxing poster served to help establish that the *Enterprise* officers had, in fact, traveled backwards in time. A trivial piece of signage would normally pass unnoted, first into the studio's trash dumpster, then into oblivion. But in this case, the image of that '30s poster, first seen by fans in 1967, would be frozen in time to reappear again in 1994—in an episode of STAR TREK: DEEP SPACE NINE.

In the third season episode, "Past Tense, Part II," Major Kira and Chief O'Brien make a number of brief sojourns into Earth's past. They are searching for Sisko, Dax and Bashir, who have disappeared in an odd transporter mishap. When the staff of DS9's art department met to discuss appropriate set-decoration materials for those time-travel sequences, they experienced a curious moment of déjà vu.

"In 'The City on the Edge of Forever,' Kirk and Spock travel through a time portal and come through a wall that has a boxing poster on it," recounts scenic artist Doug Drexler, a long-time fan of *The Original Series.* "And as we were reading the script to 'Past Tense,' we realized there was a sequence that was almost exactly the same, that took place in the same period, with Kira and O'Brien appearing practically in an alley."

In short order, the poster became the bridge between the two episodes.

Kira and O'Brien can find no trace of their missing comrades

But while fans who've read behind-the-scenes accounts of the visual in-jokes that occasionally wind up in episodes may feel that the production team lives for such opportunities—that's not the case, according to scenic art supervisor Michael Okuda. "It's generally a spontaneous thing," he explains.

"You certainly don't go looking for opportunities, not because they're not fun, but because there's just too much to do. The purpose isn't to tell jokes; the purpose is to create something that will support the episode. Whenever we think about doing something like this, we always ask ourselves whether the viewer is likely to pick up on it. If the answer is yes, then we *don't* do it, because we don't want to take away from the story. But we thought the poster would blend in seamlessly."

The ease of the poster's actual fabrication was another motivator, since time is always at a premium during preproduction. Drexler already had the appropriate reference on hand—a picture that he had found in an old magazine article. He simply redrew the poster on his computer, then had the piece fabricated at Paramount's sign shop.

Even at that, the effort might have remained a private tribute to *The Original Series,* if not for director Jonathan Frakes. While it is the art department's responsibility to make sure that there are appropriate details in the STAR TREK sets, it is ultimately the director's decision as to which details should be included in his shot.

"Sometimes the graphics make the look of the set," says Drexler. "In 'The Search,' Dax and O'Brien beam down to a Dominion relay station and it's so dark in there, that you don't see any set at all. But the graphics are lit up like Christmas trees all around and they create the whole feel of the station."

Unfortunately, there's no way to predict which graphic elements will wind up being featured by the director in any given episode, which is why the graphics team was so tickled when they saw the final version of "Past Tense."

"Jonathan Frakes really showed the poster, although I don't think he realized its significance," says Drexler. "When we saw the way he'd shot it, we were laughing. It was so great!"

Odo plays host to Curzon in a Trill rite in which Jadzia meets Dax's former hosts in "Facets"

and Rom's scandalously profit-seeking, clothes-wearing mother (aka Moogie), in an episode directed by Rene Auberjonois. Quark also finds himself "drafted" into a Klingon family when a widowed warrioress decides he must take her dead husband's place in "The House of Quark." Certainly, the adorably despicable Quark (Armin Shimerman) has his fans; Ferengophiles can be found everywhere. In fact, *The Ferengi Rules of Acquisition* by Quark (as told to Ira Steven Behr), is available from Pocket Books.

The Rules figured prominently in "Prophet Motive" (another Rene Auberjonois-directed episode), when Grand Nagus Zek (reprised brilliantly by veteran character actor Wallace Shawn) releases the new, *improved* version of the Rules. The first: "If they want their money back . . . give it to them." Even worse, the Grand Nagus has created a Ferengi Benevolent Association, believing that it's time to move "beyond greed." Fortunately, Quark learns that Zek's distressingly altruistic trans-formation is the result of a recent visit to the wormhole and the intervention of the entities who dwell within. A repeat visit convinces the prophets to restore Zek and the Ferengi status quo.

Bajoran mysticism resurfaced in "Destiny," when Benjamin Sisko's role as the Emissary of prophecy is once again confirmed, and in "Explorers," when Sisko and son attempt to prove a Bajoran legend that early space adventurers used solar sailing vessels that carried them into Cardassian territory. Bajoran theocracy figures in "Shakaar," when Kira and friend succeed in ousting the unscrupulous Kai Winn (Louise Fletcher).

In "Facets," Dax (Terry Farrell) transfers each of her former hosts' memories to one of her Deep Space Nine friends' bodies, and discovers the surprising fact that Curzon booted her out of the symbiont program because he was in love with her. (The episode provided each one of the talented cast opportunities to play a different character. Particularly noteworthy is Rene Auberjonois's performance as Curzon-Odo.)

O'Brien races against time to deactivate the Cardassian fail-safe and save Deep Space Nine

Deep Space Nine's first year introduced the mysterious Cardassian exile, Garak, who claimed to be nothing more than a "simple tailor." (The recurring role is played by Andrew Robinson, probably best known as the Scorpio Killer in *Dirty Harry*.) However, in the following year's "The Wire," we came to learn that the secretive Cardassian is anything but "simple"—in fact, he was once a member of the Obsidian Order, the brutal Cardassian version of the secret police. The third season gave us even

In one of STAR TREK's boldest episodes dealing with sexual mores, "Rejoined," Dax finds herself involved in a scientific project with Dr. Lenara Kahn (Susanna Thompson)—the widow of Torias, one of Dax's previous hosts. Trill society expressly forbids relationships with lovers of former hosts (the penalty is exile), but, even so, Dax and Lenara cannot ignore the feelings rekindled between them. The two women finally yield to a passionate embrace (but Kahn cannot take the final step that would mean exile). The episode was one of several ("Tribunal," "The Abandoned," "Improbable Cause") directed by Avery Brooks.

In *Deep Space Nine*'s fourth successful year, "we've really made an effort to push the envelope in terms of keeping the show character-oriented," says Behr. "We're not trying to do silly things, but we've not been afraid to take the show as far as we can take it. We've taken Dukat, Rom, and Garak very far—all of them going to strange and wondrous places where the audience hasn't expected them to go. We'll keep doing a mix of stories to keep the show interesting to the fans and the people who work on it."

Temporarily freed from his subspace limbo, Benjamin Sisko is thrilled to find that his son, Jake (Tony Todd) has prospered over the years in "The Visitor"

Bill Reitzel

But will *Deep Space Nine* enjoy the same seemingly immortal popularity as its predecessors? Hard to predict, but it certainly looks good.
Says Behr, "Movies? I can't answer that. But I would bet the show will go
six or seven seasons. And it will keep developing—like a shark that has
to keep moving to live. Where it will be in two or three years will be a surprise to all of us . . ."

Part Six

STAR TREK®
VOYAGER™

I n mid-1993 Paramount Television executives approached Rick Berman with the suggestion that he develop yet another series.

Berman quickly pulled Michael Piller and *The Next Generation* executive producer Jeri Taylor into the conversation. The trio's discussions resulted in STAR TREK: VOYAGER, a series that shares the same future era as *The Next Generation* and *Deep Space Nine*. The *U.S.S. Voyager*, "is transported to the edge of the galaxy, from which it would take seventy or eighty years at warp ten to get home," Berman explains.

According to Michael Piller, during series's genesis, the executive producers "asked ourselves who our captain was going to be, and we decided it might be interesting to make him a science officer." *Him?*

A scientist, yes. But at some point in the development process, the *he* became a *she:* Captain Elizabeth Janeway. Numerous actresses read for the part, including Kate Mulgrew; however, it went to Canadian film star Genevieve Bujold—who vacated the role the second day of shooting. When Bujold left, Mulgrew was called back. This time, her performance won her the role—and *Elizabeth* was rechristened Kathryn.

In *Voyager*'s pilot episode, "Caretaker," Chakotay is the captain of the Maquis vessel and a member of the people mentioned in the *The Next Generation* episode "Journey's End," a group of Native Americans who left Earth and formed their own colony. Actor Robert Beltran was cast as the calm and courageous Chakotay.

Jeff Katz

(left to right) Lieutenant Tuvok (Tim Russ), Captain Kathryn Janeway (Kate Mulgrew), and Commander Chakotay (Robert Beltran), part of the Starship Voyager command crew

Another Starfleet officer turned Maquis is Lieutenant Tom Paris, a man with a troubled past. Responsible for a tragic accident, Paris was dismissed from Starfleet and enlisted with the Maquis—only to be captured by Starfleet and imprisoned at a Federation penal facility. When Janeway recruits him for the *Voyager* crew, he accepts the chance at redemption.

The part of Tom Paris went to Robert Duncan McNeill, who ironically had played a similar character (Cadet Nicholas Locarno) in the *The Next Generation* episode "The First Duty."

Now, although *Voyager* wound up lost in the Delta quadrant so that

(top to bottom) Lieutenant Tom Paris (Robert Duncan McNeill), helmsman; Chief Engineer B'Elanna Torres (Roxann Biggs-Dawson); and Harry Kim (Garrett Wang), operations and communications officer

viewers could meet new alien races, the producers decided it was time for another Vulcan—a hundred-and-fifty-year-old security chief and captain's confidant, to be played by a fiftyish human actor.

A number of older actors read for the part, but none seemed quite right. Someone who *did* seem right was a much younger actor, Tim Russ.

Russ has a long history with STAR TREK. He guest starred on *The Next Generation* as well as *Deep Space Nine,* and as an officer aboard the *Enterprise*-B in STAR TREK GENERATIONS.

Berman had admired Russ's work for some time, and when no one else seemed to have a handle on the role of Tuvok he called in the younger actor. Russ nailed the part immediately.

Another familiarly alien face aboard the *Voyager* was B'Elanna Torres, offspring of a human father and a Klingon mother. A former Starfleet cadet, the volatile B'Elanna walked out of the academy and joined the Maquis. Roxann Biggs-Dawson managed to grasp B'Elanna's internal conflict between her cool human intellect and hot Klingon emotions.

Also on board for *Voyager*'s trek home is the first Asian cast regular since *The Original Series'* Sulu (George Takei), Ensign Harry Kim. Ops-Communications Officer Kim is a wet-behind-the-ears Academy graduate on his first mission.

One of the new aliens on board for the ride is the adorably bizarre garbage-collector-cum-chef, Neelix. By the end of the pilot, "Caretaker," the Talaxian has managed to deceive the *Voyager* crew into rescuing his

Kes (Jennifer Lien) and
Neelix (Ethan Phillips) natives
of the Delta quadrant who
volunteered their services
to help the crew of *Voyager*
find their way home

true love, Kes. Yet Neelix's manipulative streak is made up for by his generous heart and good intentions.

Neelix is utterly devoted to the young Ocampan, Kes. Trapped for many generations underground and tended to by a being known as the Caretaker, the Ocampa slowly lost their mental powers. As an Ocampan, Kes faces a life span of only nine years. Kes is as much in love with the Talaxian as he is with her.

The last crew member technically doesn't exist. When all of *Voyager*'s medical staff are killed, the emergency medical program—a holographic physician—is activated. The Doctor was such a jerk that Robert Picardo *didn't* want the role but the producers finally convinced Picardo to take the doctor's role.

Reflecting on *Voyager*'s first season, executive producer Jeri Taylor said: "The making of the pilot was definitely one of the great highlights. As we began to watch the dailies, we realized *this* cast had a chemistry that allowed them to gel immediately as an ensemble—a truly astonishing thing to see."

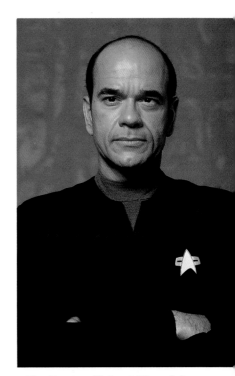

The Doctor (Robert Picardo)
is an emergency medical
hologram

213

Casting the Captain, Part III

Captain Kathryn Janeway (Kate Mulgrew)

Almost everyone involved with casting the role of the *Starship Voyager*'s Captain Janeway agrees the process was arduous. Rick Berman is philosophical about it all: "It was long and difficult when we were casting Patrick Stewart and Avery Brooks, too. This one was maybe a bit longer, maybe a bit more difficult than either one of those."

First, there was enormous pressure to find the "right" person to follow in the footsteps of Kirk, Picard, and Sisko. Guess wrong, and the STAR TREK franchise goes out the window.

Second, as Michael Piller points out, "The available pool of talent who are willing to commit to do a series is not that deep. There are a lot of actors and actresses who don't want to do episodic television for seven years."

Third, the three executive producers, Rick Berman, Michael Piller, and Jeri Taylor, were unanimous from the outset: They wanted a female. Studio executives were not so sure. Rick, Michael, and Jeri knew they could find the right woman, but the studio wanted to be convinced.

Piller recalls: "Every available actress for this part was read or spoken with. We could not find somebody we all agreed on." Either amongst the three executive producers or between the three and the studio people involved. The list of actresses called in to read for the part got longer. Examples of potential candidates included Linda Hamilton, Patsy Kensit, Kate Mulgrew, Susan Gibney, Lindsey Wagner, Chelsea Field, Kate Jackson, and Joanna Cassidy.

Finally, several candidates emerged. One was Gibney, whom Berman was particularly in favor of. "She's a marvelous actress," he says enthusiastically." The studio rejected this latest round of submissions and requested that men be considered. "So we had to go back and start the whole process over again," Piller adds.

Genevieve Bujold was suggested. She seemed to solve everyone's objections. She was attractive, the right age, an Academy Award–winning actress, had name recognition, and even had a pleasing French-Canadian accent, although she had never done episodic televison. Suddenly everyone was optimistic, enthusiastic even, that the search was over at last. Everyone, except Rick Berman.

"In meeting her, she's a very lovely lady, I immediately sensed this wasn't a person who was the slightest bit ready to live through the drudgery of episodic television. It's a grueling, vastly different world from features." He recalls, "I sat her down and said, 'I want to play devil's advocate.' I explained to her in painful detail what an absolute nightmare episodic televison is. Up at five A.M. on Mondays and Tuesdays, working till one A.M. on Thursdays and Fridays. Almost no rehearsal time. Instead of doing one or two pages of script a day like in features, she'd be doing seven or eight. Never knowing her directors, and working with them whether she liked them or not. I painted as dismal a picture as I could, even worse than it actually is, and sent her home for the weekend to think about it."

Monday morning Genevieve called Rick and said "Oui." She also had a request: Change the captain's first name to Nicole, which was Genevieve's own birth name. Elizabeth Janeway, as the Captain was then known, became Nicole Janeway. Rick called Michael and Jeri to relay the news. "But I still didn't buy it," Rick remembers. "I said, 'This ain't gonna work.' "

On the second day of shooting Genevieve called Rick and said, "I can't do this." Later, Berman would confirm that "every reason she gave me was one I had warned her about."

Two months into production Genevieve's decision would have been devastating. A day and a half in, it was a problem that could be handled. The executive producers went back through their lists. Kate Mulgrew was called in for a second reading, along with a number of others. Mulgrew made the final cut. Susan Gibney was also included—Berman wasn't ready to admit defeat. Paramount still felt Gibney was too young, and cut her from the finalists. "At that point," Berman says, "Michael, Jeri, and I all believed that Kate was the best. The studio guys agreed."

Mulgrew couldn't be happier. "I was ready for this role," she proclaims. It shows. As one of the production crew later recalled, "The moment she walked onto the set for the first time, you could actually feel the change. The Captain was on board." Piller added, "I think we got lucky. She's been a godsend for the show."

Jeri Taylor concurs. "Television is a fast-paced business. It doesn't stop for anything, or anyone. You need someone exactly like Kate Mulgrew, who is a seasoned, veteran performer . . . who understands the rigors, who understands the discipline required, who has the incredible ability to focus."

The search for *Voyager*'s captain finally came to an end. Except for one last detail: Nicole Janeway became Kathryn Janeway.

The focus of the first few episodes, says Taylor, "was to have our crew come to grips with the fact that they're seventy thousand light-years from home. In one episode, "The Cloud," Janeway had to reconsider the philosophy of command. Under normal circumstances, she might behave as a remote, detached captain, but *now* this was a family that needed closeness and bonding. The Maquis-Starfleet conflict was the focus of the first regular episode, "Parallax," in which B'Elanna Torres became chief engineer. A more internal conflict was dealt with in "Faces," in which she finds herself split into two entities: the all-Klingon B'Elanna, and the all-human Torres.

In "Eye of the Needle," the *Voyager* crew discovers a wormhole that leads them to an encounter with a Romulan captain in the Alpha quadrant. The episode "worked nicely," Taylor says, calling it "the first of our 'we might have a way to get home' stories. It seemed to resonate with the poignancy and the longing of these people to get home" and their frustration at the "cruel, unexpected twist of fate" when it's discovered the Romulan can only return them to the past. " 'Prime Factors' was a show we were very proud of," she continues. Torres and (astoundingly) the Vulcan Tuvok decide to illegally obtain a device that might help them return home when legal efforts fail. "It put B'Elanna and Tuvok in a situation where they had to break the rules, and Janeway had to decide how to deal with this breach of her authority."

B'Elanna Torres is torn in two beings, one human and one Klingon, by a twisted medical experiment of the Vidiians in "Faces"

The Doctor goes off on his first "away mission" in "Heroes and Demons"—to the holodeck, to rescue Kim, Chakotay, and Tuvok from a *Beowulf* scenario gone awry. Soon he finds himself in a startling new set-

Starship Voyager

STAR TREK VOYAGER *Technical Manual (created by and for the Voyager production staff)* states, "The *U.S.S. Voyager* is the newest Federation starship. It is an Intrepid-class vessel, one of the fastest and most powerful in the fleet." The ship is much smaller—about half the length—than Picard's *Enterprise*, "carries a crew complement of about 150 (no families), is capable of independent operation for about three years without refueling, and can sustain speeds of up to warp 9.2 for periods of up to eight hours."

The design of *Voyager* was a collaborative effort, beginning with Executive Producer Rick Berman all the way down to the men and women who actually put pen to the paper (or bytes on the disk). But the man ultimately responsible for guiding and shaping *Voyager's* evolution is the series's Emmy Award–winning production designer, Richard James.

"Rick wanted a sleeker design, more bullet-shaped, so that's where I started," James recalls. "I began with two basic teams at first—one working on the bridge and interiors, the other working on the exterior." Part of the task facing James and his teams was to maintain a STAR TREK "look," while creating something obviously different, more advanced in appearance.

Mike Okuda, *Voyager's* scenic arts supervisor, elaborated: "We felt strongly that one of the things that should drive the design of *Voyager* was to build upon the design of the *Enterprise,* which is one of the most recognizable icons in American television." This sentiment was echoed by Rick Sternbach, *Voyager's* senior illustrator: "The design challenge was to make it as different as possible from the *Enterprise* while still being a recognizable cousin."

In meeting that challenge, James instructed his staff to consider all possibilities, no matter how far out. For the exterior of the ship, James said, "I wanted to know how many design elements we could change and still achieve our goal. Can we reshape the saucer? Can we eliminate it? Can we rearrange the engines? How can we play with the

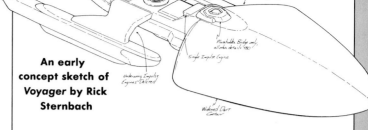

An early concept sketch of Voyager by Rick Sternbach

symmetry?" Inside, James focused on the bridge at first. "Once we got Rick Berman's approval on the bridge design, that became the driving influence for the design of the rest of the interiors."

Regular STAR TREK viewers will immediately notice significant changes from the *Enterprise* bridge to the *Voyager* bridge. *Voyager's* bridge is more elaborate, has a more "tech" feel to it, incorporates eleven video monitors, and utilizes an expanded multilevel layout for crew positions. "We also made the main view screen smaller," James explained. "When the camera is in for a close-up you don't know how big it is. Besides, the view screen is a wild wall [movable], so a smaller view screen is a lot easier to move in and out of position for shooting."

Utilizing three-dimensional sketches at first, James and Berman guided the initial efforts until Berman was satisfied they were on the right track. The next step was to build prototype models of both the ship and the standing sets. "After that, it was a process of elimination and refining more than anything else," James added. Once the exterior of the ship was finalized, the shooting model was built by renowned model maker Tony Meininger.

One of the ship's most striking exterior aspects is the articulating engine nacelles, which move upward to a 45-degree position as *Voyager* prepares to accelerate to warp speed. This is, according to the series's "bible," part of a "new technology which allows the ship to fly at warp speed without damaging the fabric of space." Another innovation—without precedent for STAR TREK starships—is *Voyager's* ability to land and take off again from planet surfaces.

The result of Production Designer James's vision is a uniquely fresh starship visually related to its STAR TREK predecessors, but just as obviously possessing its own distinctive identity. The evolution of that identity began in May of 1993, and was continuing even as *Voyager* premiered in January of 1995. "I'm glad it's turned out the way it has," James summarizes. "That's part of my job, to use the talents and skills of the people on my staff, keep the designs on track, and make everything look like it came from the same source."

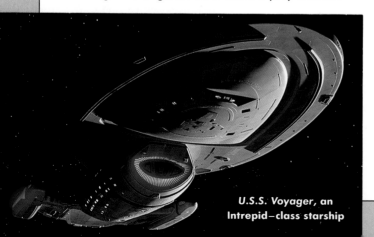

U.S.S. Voyager, an Intrepid–class starship

ting, surrounded by Norse Woodlands and blonde Viking maidens.

The first season's last episode, "Learning Curve," shows Tuvok's struggle to turn a group of Maquis rebels into disciplined Starfleet officers. The Vulcan's efforts are met with sullen resentment. However, a crisis convinces them that maybe they can work together.

Taylor points out that "Learning Curve" was *"not* the episode we would have chosen to end the season with." United Paramount Network decided to withhold the series's last four shows and run them the following season.

The episode designed to be the final episode was "The 37s," which instead wound up being the second season's opener. The *Voyager* crew stumbles upon a distress call emanating from a group of humans, all abducted from Earth in 1937. The show also marked *Voyager*'s landing— a first for STAR TREK.

"Initiations," which was intended as the second season's premiere, featured a confrontation between Chakotay and a young Kazon (Kar, played by DEEP SPACE NINE's Aron Eisenberg) determined to kill as part of a maturity ritual. VOYAGER continues the tradition of providing insight and respect for "the enemy's" point of view, as the episode gives us

Respect, trust, and admiration have built strong bonds between Chakotay and Janeway, so that the captain feels free to discuss her fears in "The 37s"

a glimpse inside the Kazon culture. "Projections" featured the Doctor (with guest star Dwight Schulz), who is activated during a shipwide emergency only to discover that *he* is real and everyone else on board is apparently a holograph.

The episode "Persistence of Vision" is noteworthy in that it explored the characters' personal lives and conflicts. The show "began Janeway on a journey she needs to take," Taylor says, "which is resolving the matter of her lover, Mark. We cannot put her into romantic situations until she decides he has given her up for dead and moved on, and the only wise thing for her to do is the same." Other notable second-season episodes include "Manuevers," in which the treacherous Seska (Chakotay's former intimate) joins with the Kazon in an effort to take over the *Voyager*; and "Resistance," in which an Alsaurian eccentric (Caylem, played by Broadway veteran Joel Grey) kidnaps Janeway under the delusion that she is his daughter.

The second season's emphasis, Taylor notes, is to "focus on one character and get under his or her skin—to find out what makes these people tick." She adds: "One of the things we felt after last season was

Tuvok takes up the challenge of teaching members of the Maquis Starfleet discipline in ''Learning Curve''

The Enemy Within: The Maquis

B'Elenna Torres (Roxann Biggs-Dawson) and Seska (Martha Hackett), former members of the Marquis

The origins of the Maquis date back to *Voyager*'s earliest developmental discussions. As Michael Piller recalls, "Rick Berman, Jeri Taylor, and I asked ourselves, 'What will make this an interesting crew?' The answer for us was to find ourselves chasing an outlaw group. We all get tossed onto the other side of the galaxy and everybody has to team up in order to survive."

Once the executive producers agreed on the premise, the next step was to create an identity for the outlaw group. Rick Berman was particularly concerned that the group not be too cutthroat. He wanted *less* inherent conflict among *Voyager*'s crew than there is on *Deep Space Nine*. Berman believed that ultimately these people needed to become a tightly bonded crew.

The search for the outlaw group's identity and name led to a group of French resistance fighters during World War II—the Maquis. Jeri Taylor explains: "Rick wanted to preserve the idea of a noble cause behind the Maquis's criminal activities. We created a Cardassian-Federation treaty in which there are colonies caught in the middle. They are not willing to compromise their principles for the sake of political harmony between two distant governments."

Voyager's *Writer's-Directors' Guide* provides additional insight: "The Cardassians and the Federation consider the Maquis outlaws, but in their own minds they are freedom fighters. They are idealistic non–conformists who believe passionately that they are taking the only course of action they can take to protect themselves from Cardassian aggression."

The next step was to make them familiar to STAR TREK viewers. In mid-1993, eighteen months before *Voyager* debuted, work began on four Maquis-oriented episodes. Two were aired on *The Next Generation* and two on *Deep Space Nine*. By the time *Voyager* premiered, with the Starfleet crew in pursuit of a Maquis ship, viewers were familiar with the Maquis.

In the months leading up to *Voyager*'s premiere this mix of personnel was widely discussed in the press. In such a situation, inevitably, there would be tension, even arguments. Dissension on the bridge of a Starfleet vessel? Many thought the idea was tantamount to blasphemy.

The *Writers'-Directors' Guide* attempts to clarify the issue: "Most Maquis share a common trait: they are not comfortable living under the strict rules of conduct demanded by Starfleet. They are independent, free-thinking individuals with perhaps a few more rough edges than we might see in a typical Starfleet crew. As the series evolves, we will expect to see fewer rough edges and less frequent conflict."

Maybe so, but the *potential* for conflict is still there.

Rick Berman was determined to avoid creating a mixed crew that would constantly be banging heads. "We were looking for a middle ground here," Berman affirms. "We wanted to get the Maquis into Starfleet uniforms, with a captain who had to pull together diverse groups of people into a functioning, solid, effective unit. It would get pretty irritating, and cumbersome, to have Maquis tension in every episode. But it comes up often during the course of each season."

Clearly, certain *Voyager* episodes would be impossible without the Maquis. An example is the second-season episode "Meld," in which, while conducting a murder investigation, Tuvok mind–melds with a sociopathic killer who is a Maquis. Michael Piller: "The whole story is based on the fact that nobody really knows about the backgrounds of these Maquis. The murderer is a man who joined the Maquis because he really, really likes to kill. Finally he kills somebody aboard *Voyager*.

"If we had no Maquis on the ship you would never find a Starfleet officer—one who's successfully completed the training—who would murder. So, there are stories to be told because of the Maquis background, and they are coming out. It's just not every week."

The "Enemy Within?" Perhaps. But the Maquis, integrated with a Starfleet crew, seems more fittingly viewed as yet another facet of Gene Roddenberry's original vision of the future: infinite diversity in infinite combinations.

Now, Chakotay proudly wears Starfleet's uniform

The Doctor tries to determine if he's married and trapped in a holodeck, or if he's a hologram on a lost starship in "Projections"

that we hadn't fully explored Tom Paris. We wanted to make him more heroic, and so we've come up with a new multiple-episode arc. Each show ("Alliances," "Threshhold," "Meld," "Dreadnaught," and "Investigations") stands alone, but there's a continuing thread in which we posit a spy on *Voyager,* and then posit the notion that Paris has begun to chafe under Starfleet regulations. He asks to leave the ship. What we ultimately discover is that all of this has been a ruse to find out the identity of the spy."

With the success of STAR TREK GENERATIONS and more *The Next Generation* films on the horizon, plus the staying power of *Deep Space Nine,* STAR TREK seems truly immortal. But Jeri Taylor is quick to point out: "We stay on the edges of our seats (at *Voyager*); we haven't become complacent. We're very mindful of the fact that we have to come up with the very best we can offer, if we're to live up to what has gone before in STAR TREK."

Realizing they are walking into a trap, Janeway pulls Caylem (Joel Grey) back into the safety of the shadows in "Resistance"

Appendix

Star Trek: The Motion Pictures

Film #	Title	Stardate
1	Star Trek: The Motion Picture	7412.6
2	Star Trek II: The Wrath of Khan	8130.3
3	Star Trek III: The Search for Spock	8210.3
4	Star Trek IV: The Voyage Home	8390.0

Production #	Title	Stardate
5	Star Trek V: The Final Frontier	8454.1
6	Star Trek VI: The Undiscovered Country	9521.6
7	Star Trek: Generations:	
	Enterprise B Timeline	9715.0
	Enterprise D Timeline	48650.1

Star Trek: The Animated Series

Production #	Title	Stardate
SEASON ONE		
1	Yesteryear	5373.4
2	One of Our Planets Is Missing	5371.3
3	The Lorelai Signal	5483.7
4	More Tribbles, More Troubles	5392.4
5	The Survivor	5143.3
6	The Infinite Vulcan	5554.4
7	The Magicks of Megas-tu	1254.4
8	Once Upon a Planet	5591.2
9	Mudd's Passion	4978.5
10	The Terratin Incident	5577.3
11	Time Trap	5267.2
12	The Ambergris Element	5499.9

Production #	Title	Stardate
13	Slaver Weapon	4187.3
14	Beyond the Farthest Star	5521.3
15	The Eye of the Beholder	5501.2
16	Jihad	5683.1
SEASON TWO		
17	The Pirates of Orion	6334.1
18	BEM	7403.6
19	Practical Joker	3183.3
20	Albatross	5275.6
21	How Sharper Than a Serpent's Tooth	6063.4
22	The Counter-Clock Incident	6770.3

Star Trek: The Next Generation

Paramount Pictures designated the first episode of STAR TREK: THE NEXT
GENERATION as production number 101 to differentiate *The Next Generation*
episodes from the production numbers for episodes of
STAR TREK: THE ORIGINAL SERIES.

Production #	Title	Stardate
SEASON ONE		
101	Encounter at Farpoint, Part 1	41153.7
102	Encounter at Farpoint, Part 2	41153.7
103	The Naked Now	41209.2
104	Code of Honor	41235.5
105	Haven	41294.5
106	Where No One Has Gone Before	41263.1
107	The Last Outpost	41386.4
108	Lonely Among Us	41249.3
109	Justice	41255.6
110	The Battle	41723.9
111	Hide And Q	41590.5
112	Too Short a Season	41309.5
113	The Big Goodbye	41997.7
114	Datalore	41242.4
115	Angel One	41636.9
116	11001001	41365.9
117	Home Soil	41463.9
118	When the Bough Breaks	41509.1
119	Coming of Age	41416.2
120	Heart of Glory	41503.7
121	The Arsenal of Freedom	41798.2
122	Skin of Evil	41601.3
123	Symbiosis	No Stardate

Production #	Title	Stardate
124	We'll Always Have Paris	41679.9
125	Conspiracy	41775.5
126	The Neutral Zone	41986.0
SEASON TWO		
127	The Child	42073.1
128	Where Silence Has Lease	42193.6
129	Elementary, Dear Data	42286.3
130	The Outrageous Okona	42402.7
131	The Schizoid Man	42437.5
132	Loud as a Whisper	42477.2
133	Unnatural Selection	42494.8
134	A Matter of Honor	42506.5
135	The Measure of a Man	42523.7
136	The Dauphin	42568.8
137	Contagion	42609.1
138	The Royale	42625.4
139	Time Squared	42679.2
140	The Icarus Factor	42686.4
141	Pen Pals	42695.3
142	Q Who?	42761.3
143	Samaritan Snare	42779.1
144	Up the Long Ladder	42823.2

PHOTO CREDITS

ABOUT THE AUTHOR

J.M. Dillard is the author of several bestselling STAR TREK® novels, including THE LOST YEARS and the novelizations of STAR TREK V: THE FINAL FRONTIER™, STAR TREK VI: THE UNDISCOVERED COUNTRY™, STAR TREK® GENERATIONS™, and STAR TREK: DEEP SPACE NINE®: EMISSARY. She currently lives in a small California town with her husband, two bird dogs, and a bird.